Blue Jewellery

THE
SEAGULL
LIBRARY OF
GERMAN
LITERATURE

Blue Jewellery

Katharina Winkler

TRANSLATED BY LAURA WAGNER

LONDON NEW YORK CALCUTTA

This publication has been supported by a grant from
the Goethe-Institut India

Seagull Books, 2022

Originally published in German as *Blauschmuck*
© Suhrkamp Verlag, Berlin, 2016

First published in English translation by Seagull Books, 2018
English translation © Laura Wagner, 2018

Published as part of the Seagull Library of German Literature, 2022

ISBN 978 1 8030 9 002 3

British Library Cataloguing-in-Publication Data
A catalogue record for this book is available from the British Library.

Typeset by Seagull Books, Calcutta, India
Printed and bound by WordsWorth India, New Delhi, India

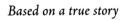

Based on a true story

Our group of children forms a herd.

The hay is our bed. The smell of cut summer. We lie across and atop one another. Who can say who this foot or that hand belongs to.

Mother?

We breathe deeply. We smell of the past day.

Of sweat, of sun. We fart into one another's faces.

I hear them say that we are ten children. I hear them say that I am the seventh.

Like a cow my mother drops children, one after the other, between sowing and harvest and sowing. Big and heavy she stands in the noonday heat and tends the hay. Between two haystacks, a child then falls from her lap. A girl, a boy, a girl, a boy, a girl, a boy, like pearls on a string.

Just once it was a boy after another boy, but he died, and then a girl came right after.

There are also other herds of children on our hills.

Our names are Aliye, Hüseyin, Fatma, Mehmet, Yıldız, Ali, Filiz, Sayit, Zehra, Remzi, Selin, Veli.

Goats, kids, sheep, lambs, children, cows, calves, donkey, horse. We all are herd and shepherds at the same time. We herd one another. Nurture one another and hit each other in the flanks. Mother protects us from Father, Father protects us from wolves and we children protect each other like the sheep and lambs and goats and kids protect one another, Hüseyin and Mehmet herd the cows, Sayit and Zehra the goats, Yıldız the sheep.

I herd the lambs.

Wolves come flying over the hill, one after the other, six, seven, a pack. They lunge for the sheep, teeth first, rip up the prey, guts and stomachs full of grass, rip the flesh from each other's mouths, trembling skeletons prancing among the kill.

Feeding.

The wolves eat the sheep. They gut them. They rummage around in their intestines.

Lungs, bowels, liver, spleen, heart.

Dying is red. Blood on white wool. Blood on green meadow. Blood trails, streaks of blood, dripping, flowing, pouring blood.

When the wolf pack retreats, the flies come.

Black clouds above the dead.

Yıldız is suddenly standing among the sheep. Her black plait is dripping, still wet from playing at the stream.

Father is going to beat me to death! Father is going to beat me to death!

And:

Filiz! Filiz!

As if I knew what to do. I sense behind me:

3

Father. See him in Yıldız's face. He runs up the hill, lifts his tanned hands and cries desperately: Allah!

On the battlefield lies the tea, the sugar, the salt for the animals, lie the clothes for the coming year.

Father calls for the sons. Hüseyin and Mehmet run to him and curse and wail: Allah! Then they throw the carcasses onto wheelbarrows.

In wheelbarrows, the dead jolt back to the stable.

Yıldız has disappeared.

The rest of the family gathers in the stable, guts the animals.

Mother laments the bloodstained wool that she can neither wash nor dye white any more.

When it gets dark, Father goes looking for Yıldız. Menacingly, he walks through the stable and across the field. Yıldız has pressed herself into the bushes like a rabbit.

When Father spots her, she runs away, chases across the field, across the hills, into the darkness of the meadow and bolts up a tree.

Father gestures threateningly towards the branches, tries to climb up, falls, curses, falls.

Dawn is coming as Father goes back to the house, to his bed. That's where Mother sleeps. With open eyes. She waits until Father's breathing is deep and steady, then she dares to go to the tree. She hands Yıldız food into the branches:

Stay where you are.

From my bed, I see the sister between the branches in the moonlit night.

The next day, we eat fried mutton.

We share our meat with the wolves.

When Father enters the house, he brings the silence with him.

We rise, our eyes coordinating with each other, Yıldız moves a chair behind Father, Fatma takes his jacket off his shoulders, I hurry into the kitchen to the barrel, scoop water into a bowl, three full ladles. Fatma is crouching down in front of Father, has untied his shoelaces, pulls the right shoe off the heel, I crouch down next to her and take the left one, Father's foot is damp and warm. I dip it into the cool water and wash the day off his soles. Zehra hands me the towel, I rub the foot dry and let it slide from my hand and into the sandal.

Mother has been baking. We have flatbread with beans and cheese and fresh ayran.

During the meal, we sit silently. Just as Father wants us.

Honour stands above everything else, Father says.

The sun alights from honour.

Honour lets us sleep peacefully.

We breathe it. In and out.

At night and during the day.

Honour has to thrive on our fields.

We eat it, and the women nurse their children with it.

Honour is the most important thing to my father.

More important than us children. Or Mother.

Honour stands above everything else, Father says.

Honour outgrows me.

We have six gardens. There are potatoes, onions, cucumbers, tomatoes and bell peppers, beans and lettuce, sweetcorn and basil, melons, chickpeas and cabbage. Apples, pears, apricots, mulberries, plums, grapes.

Our plot of land is stony. The neighbour's garden is bigger and lusher.

The neighbour's fruit is ours, Mother says, Grandfather planted it.

When Father was young, the neighbours called a bailiff from Kiğı and declared the garden theirs.

Father sat at their table and nodded silently towards the faces of the neighbour's four sons.

Father didn't have any brothers, so they put down the law.

The bailiff measured out the plot of land and recorded what was dictated to him.

After that, the neighbours filled the glasses and drank with Father, toasting good neighbourship.

When the mulberries in the garden are red, us children steal back our property and the red juice flows down our chins.

What we can't eat, we collect in baskets and bring to Mother. We dry the summer, store it in our cellar and eat it in winter.

We share the stream with the neighbours. Nine days a month it flows for us. The other days, the neighbours channel it to their fields and their gardens. Then, we wait for the stream.

Long before it arrives, I can hear its rushing.

One morning, we flipped the wooden lever and waited. The stream didn't come. The garden's green was brittle. With dry gums, Hüseyin, Fatma and I walked up the dusty riverbed. The neighbours further up had stolen the stream and directed it into their garden. Their tomatoes were red like the evening sky.

When we told Mother, she became furious, gasping for breath, she stomped up the hill across the brown meadows, her clamour driving the neighbours from their house, the curses rolling down the hill. My father hurried from the stables, upwards across the hill, in order to save his honour. Behind the hill, Aylin appeared, the thieves' daughter, I waved at her, she waved back at me.

Days later, Mother and the neighbour's wife are chatting in our kitchen as though there was water enough. It's people that are rare in these parts.

On hot days, we sleep outside. Seven children on mattresses filled with hay. Swarms of flies lay siege to our mouths and to the corners of our eyes. Mother starts a fire and burns dried cow dung. With her apron, she fans the smoke into our faces. That chases away the flies, she says. Sayit waggles his feet in front of my face.

They reek of cow dung, he laughs, that also chases away the flies.

Sleep! Mother's voice falls onto his giggles, we have to get up early the next morning, there's plenty of work to do.

Behind the smoke, the stars are sparkling.

The brightest of them is mine.

There are a hundred blue women living in our valley. There are light blue women like Necla's mother and dark blue women like Fidan's mother, there are red-blue women and black-blue ones. There are women who carry their blue around their necks like a necklace or in the hollow below the neck like a locket, some carry their blue like a bracelet, some around their ankles.

Many women change their blue jewellery from week to week, some day to day. Some smile constantly, despite their blue jewellery, like Leyla, some keep silent in blue, like Zehra.

Light-blue women become dark-blue ones, red-blue ones become black-blue ones. Dark-blue ones also become light blue, but that's rare, and women who wear black blue, like Ayşe, don't ever let go of the heavy colour.

There are women whose blue jewellery no one knows, women who hide it underneath long clothes, beneath scarves, blue girls usually like Elif and Selin who still wear their blue anxiously, like lipstick for the first time.

The women's blue jewellery bears the hallmarks of men. The tools, wood or iron, and the number of blows determine the shade of blue.

The blue women wear the colour of the sky. Cloud-streaked summer sky, icy winter sky, fickle spring sky, grey autumn sky, dusk, rainbow.

Only Songül is skyless and without blue. Wherever she appears, conversation stops.

What could you talk about with the skyless.

She walks through the village with unblemished skin. The women turn away, no word, no greeting to the skyless. Look at her! Says my mother and strokes my hair with her blue-black hand, neither smart nor diligent. And still: not a single blue spot!

There are people like that too, she says, unfortunately.

When I grow up, I will be a blue woman.

I'm hoping for a shade of blue as light as the winter sky.

Mother thinks that I am six years old, Yıldız reckons that I'm seven already. I'm tall, everyone can see that, tall enough to herd: the lambs, my sister Selin and my virgin.

I know the lambs well. I know what they eat and drink.

I know Selin well. I know that she laughs when I stroke across her forehead with a poppy.

I don't know my virgin. But she lives within me and I mustn't lose her. I have to protect her and give my life for her if necessary, Father says. I mustn't chew gum, that I know. Aylin got pregnant from a chewing gum her uncle brought her from the city. Lemons, Yıldız says, I mustn't eat either, they colour the red virgin white. I have lain awake at night before and was afraid that there had been lemon in the neighbour's stew.

I'm scared of the dark, because the dark impregnates. The darkness in the forest and on the meadow especially. The darkness in the valley. And the window in the kitchen is open during the night! I don't know where the darkness of the meadow ends and the darkness of our house begins. Does the darkness of the meadow flow through the kitchen window and further along the corridor and into my chamber?

We're hanging the laundry, Yıldız, Mother and I, we have washed it white. Hassan comes hopping out of the stable, young and strong like a horse.

Come! he yells, Hüseyin, Mehmet!

The boys want to go to the stream. Longing for water.

Father is standing in the doorway. The field?

Hüseyin nods. Done!

The boys start running. Father looks after them.

Then he goes to the field. The clods are gleaming in the sun. With the tip of his shoe, Father brushes through the fresh soil. He bends down and swipes through the furrow.

Not deep enough.

Just like the next furrow. And the one after that.

The soil on which bread is to grow for the family!

Hüseyin!

Father's cry reaches all the way to the water, the boys come running, the stream still in their hair and eyelashes, Father is standing in front of the stable now, a piece of wood in his hand.

Fury has gripped my father.

He roars and beats Hüseyin, first to the floor and then into unconsciousness.

We're standing next to the wall of the house, Mehmet, Yıldız, Ali, Selin, Mother and I, and look on without moving. Looking at the brother. At Father.

Blow. After blow.

That's when Mother is jolted from her paralysis, Mehmet throws himself between them, wrestling with Father for the piece of wood, Mother rushes over to Hüseyin and pulls the lifeless son onto her lap as though she wanted to give birth to him once more. She rocks him back and forth and puts her hand on his forehead.

She sings him a lullaby.

Father cowers next to the destroyed son, silently.

Later, Hüseyin awakens.

He sees his ribcage, his arms and legs, and cries with shame.

Blue jewellery is only meant for women.

The fun! The fun!

Mother often talks about the fun she once had in a winter's night long gone. She is rubbing the laundry on the board.

One time, I was a wild one.

It was during a night in the first winter. My new-lywed father awoke, he felt around for his wife, but the bed was empty. He called out for her, but she didn't come, he called again, no answer. He got up, walked through the house, when he suddenly heard her laugh. He saw her through the window in the glistening snow, on the snow mountain he had scooped off the stable's roof, the headscarf had slipped down to her shoulders, hair in disarray, head thrown back, from her open mouth with the full lips, white breath billowing from deep within her chest, the skirt had risen up above her knees, her legs straddling a burlap sack and she was laughing. She pushed herself off the mountain peak with glowing white calves, skidded down the snow mountain whooping with joy, spun out of control, cheering even while falling, tumbled over herself, slid further, stayed on the ground laughing in the snow.

My father pulled her into the stable by the hair, beat her head against the wall until blood ran into her loosened hair, along her neck and across the full lips into her open mouth. Then he took his wife back into his bed.

I'm dreaming.

My mother is galloping over the hills behind our house, mane waving. Her nostrils are flared, her ears pricked up, I get in her way. Her big eyes are panicked, she looks at me, for a long time, turns on her hind legs and flees.

My sister Yıldız loves to ride horses. She sits in the saddle like a man, wind her hair, in her clothes. The men's looks are flying behind her. Soon she will be too much of a woman to gallop, my father will get in her way, he will grab the reins, will pull her off the horse and send her to the kitchen. That's where she is going to help Mother, and the wind will fall from her clothes.

The other side of the mountain is where the letters and numbers are.

With the satchel on my back, I have to cross the mountain pass every day. When Father, Mother and Hüseyin go to the stable, I climb up the mountain. I have a two-hour walk ahead of me.

There are two classes. One for the children in Grades One to Three. Another for the children in Grades Four and Five. We have two teachers. They herd us and teach us what we need for life. In the morning, when I open my notebook, I'm full of joy because I'm allowed to learn from Mister Barzan and Mister Gülabi. I like the numbers and the letters. I'm grateful that they come to me, to Yedisu. Come from far away. Even though I am young and a girl. I like the A and the Ş. Sometimes I write all twenty-nine letters in one line. I want to wrap them up as a gift and send them to Mother and Grandmother. Together they would untie the bow and the letters would jump from the box and walk out of the kitchen alongside them. But then I become scared that the letters could forget me and I whisper to them: Me! Take me! Take me with you!

I'm also friends with the numbers. I make an effort with them and soon I know them better than any other child in my class. I find numbers everywhere. None of them belongs to me. I don't know how old I am. Father couldn't walk all the way to Kiğı for every single child in order to have it registered. He only went for every second or third one. But there are letters that belong to me. I have a name. Even a surname. And that's more than what my mother had when she was a child. My grandfather gave the surname to our family as a gift. On Atatürk's command. Atatürk wanted for all Turks to carry a surname. Grandfather went to the ministry department and had them put on record: My name is now Lale. And so my name is Filiz Lale. I'm about ten years old.

Learning is important. I hear that daily.

Here in school, I learn for life.

Mister Gülabi and Mister Barzan are going to open the door to a better life for us!

I'm diligent. I read the chalk lines on the blackboard. I breathe the chalk dust. I don't want to miss anything that's important for the better life.

I sit in my seat quietly and already have opened the natural history book. The deep-sea anglerfish has the ability to create light for itself. Hassan whispers something to Musa, Musa is still giggling when Mister Barzan enters the classroom.

Musa falls silent.

Mister Barzan walks up to the teacher's table, opens the drawer, grabs his cane. We stand up and hold our hands out to him.

Each one of us picks a spot in the room on which to fasten their eyes and their soul, the wardrobe hook next to the door, the door handle, or the window catch.

Mister Barzan approaches us, cane in hand.

One blow on the last joints of the fingers.

One blow on the joints closer to the hand.

One blow on the back of the hands.

One blow on the wrist.

Our hands swell up, we keep a straight face. Only Esma's sobs are our sign of life.

We're still holding out our hands.

My gaze is fixed upon the deep-sea anglerfish.

I try to create light for myself.

Mister Barzan hits everyone.

Selin, Fidan, Elif, Fatma, Veli, Zehra, Hatun, Hanem, Remzi, Resul, Zeki, Hülya, me, Müslüm, Nurten, Feride, Fidan, Halil, Necla, Berfin, Seda, Ali, Sayit, Dilber, Elif, Mehmet, Hassan, Musa, Seda, Ayşe, Aynur, Besime, Hatice, Ahmet, Şengül, Zarife, Selin.

It must be nice to bathe in the stream.

I'm standing at the riverbank, the noonday heat on my shoulders, I'm watching the boys, those big, happy frogs that jump into the cool and still have that luminous green in their eyes when they get out of the water.

My body longs for water.

I lie down on the ground and imagine swimming. The pebbles underneath my feet are cold, the water is washing around my legs, splashing onto my belly, onto the neck, that's when a shadow falls on me, eyes upon mine: Yunus.

Almost naked, the suntanned skin full of glistening drops of water.

I can see muscles underneath the skin, bluish veins and sinews in the back of the knee. I see the impression of his member in his wet, blue pants. His hair is full, darker than black, his eyes are green from the stream. The large feet stand sturdy.

You're mine.

His voice is without doubt.

Without a word, he takes me by the hand. I go with him. I hold on to his large feet, his steps, his dark hair and his assertive gaze, don't have to hold myself up because he is holding me.

We don't say a word.

Above his right eyelid, a birthmark shines.

Yunus opens the stable door, pushes me into the empty stable, because I am his.

I have to stay here, mustn't watch any other man swim from now on.

The stable door snaps shut.

I'm standing in the dark. Trembling.

I belong to him. I have a man.

I giggle, watch his strong legs through the crack of the door, his straight back, his flawless, thirteen-year-old body that is walking away from me.

I'm staying here. I will not watch another man swim ever again.

I'm his.

I think that I'll be eleven years old this summer.

I ask Yıldız and Aylin to accompany me on a pilgrimage to the holy tree so that we may see our future husbands in a dream.

The holy tree is an hours' walk from our house. It has healed many people. My mother among them. Shortly after Hüseyin's birth, an ulcer began growing behind her left ear. At first it was white and soft, then became harder and shiny red. Mother grew weaker and weaker, and her fever rose and rose, the children were clinging to her, one in the front, one in the back and with sweat on her brow she fed the cows and the sheep and worked on the field. She couldn't move her head, neither twist nor turn it, and she prayed to Allah. One morning, she put on her clothes and left the house, taking her children with her. For hours, she dragged herself and the children to the holy tree. My mother drank from the spring close to the root, washed her wound, covered it with earth and hung a piece of cloth in the branches asking for healing. The next night, when she was half asleep, she dreamt of a snake. It wound itself up her legs and up to her neck, rammed its teeth into mother's ulcer and drained the sickness from her blood. The next day my mother awoke: healthy.

So. So we make a pilgrimage to the holy tree. So we can see our future husbands through it. We have empty bottles with us, as well as pieces of fabric that have our wish written on them: We want to know the man with whom we are going to spend our life. We hang the fabric into the branches. Our question blows in the wind.

We fill the bottles with water from the spring, carry them home. There, we bake bread with the holy water, bread that we oversalt and eat in the evening without drinking anything. The man who gives us water in our dream will be our husband.

I go to bed excitedly.

I'm dreaming.

The noonday heat is oppressive, no bird sounds.

I'm stacking wood in the courtyard, and that's when the gate opens silently, and standing in the shadow is Yunus.

He smiles at me and holds a bottle of water out to me. I'm excited and happy and smile at him and reach for the water, he laughs and pulls it away from me.

My sleep breaks.

Fluttering wings. Humming up to the neck.

I get up, walk on tiptoes, get the big glass and fill it to the brim with water and finally quench my thirst.

Once I get aybaşı, Mother says one day, I will have to be careful because no one can see it.

Aybaşı.

Mother's eyebrows are lifted, with a dark gaze she paints the word into my imagination. I don't know what aybaşı is, so I ask Yıldız, who laughs. Aybaşı you'll get for free, she says. From whom, I ask, and she laughs and doesn't give me an answer.

Aybaşı.

I search for it in gestures, smells and colours, but aybaşı doesn't show itself to me.

Aybaşı. No colour, no taste.

Leyla is beautiful. Leyla's gaze goes out into the distance.

I like playing with her. We collect treasures, gold and diamonds, stones that reflect the trees or the clouds, strange pieces of wood in which ghosts live, autumn leaves.

We exchange things. A plum stone polished by water for a piece of bark crumbling into sand.

One day, Leyla has disappeared.

Much later, I see Leyla through the window of the classroom. She is wearing loose-fitting clothes that I don't recognize. Underneath them a ball.

People point their fingers at her, the devil. They whisper.

Guilt, they say, is what Leyla is carrying in her belly.

Leyla walks through the village as though she were walking through fire.

I'm looking for coloured stones for Leyla at the stream, I want to bring them to her.

No, Mother says and takes the jewels from me, don't talk to Leyla any more.

Her hand pats my hair softly, Leyla didn't take care of her virgin.

The birds' twittering has burnt up by noon. Silence.

I walk to the spring with two buckets. For the sixth time that day. Today, the animals need more than I can carry. I fill the buckets at the stream.

Yunus.

He is handsome. Tall. Blocks the sun.

I don't move.

Promise that you will marry me!

The sunlight behind his head, a wreath of light that blinds me. I put my hand up in front of my eyes.

I promise.

That night I wake up and know: He is gone.

On the way to his uncle in Germany he has stepped right over me.

I am going to be his wife. His woman.

I am going to bake baklava for him and set the table.

I am going to milk his cows and give birth to his children and carry his name:

Şahin. Filiz Şahin.

At wedding parties, I am going to sit next to him, and when they play a song that we like, we are going to dance.

Filiz and Yunus Şahin. What a beautiful couple!

I am going to be wearing a shimmering dress and our children are already going to be asleep. I am going to be radiantly beautiful by his side. And all the girls are going to admire and envy me.

I feel a drop on my thigh. I reach underneath my skirt, feel around for it. It looks like blood. I rub it between my fingers, it colours my skin red, I smell it, it smells like slaughter. My virgin! My virgin is running out from between my legs, runs down my thighs, drips onto the floor, seeps into the sand. I know, Father, without my virgin I have nothing to expect from anybody! I run home, look for Yıldız, find her in the kitchen, drag her into the chamber, slam the door shut behind us, fall to her feet. I tell her about my virgin and hide my red-stained finger in my lap.

It's not my fault, I scream in a whisper, no man has touched me, Yıldız, I swear!

That can't be true! You've got to have done something with a man!

No, I haven't, no, I swear!

Then I remember that my uncle had kissed me, two weeks earlier, on the cheek, I hadn't wanted him to, but he was quick, quicker than I could realize, quicker than I could put up defences, so my uncle, my uncle has taken my virgin and my honour, yes, my uncle has touched me. So I am shame.

Better to die than to bring shame to my family.

Now Yıldız is laughing out loud, right in my face:

That's what Mother was talking about. Aybaşı!

From now on, you'll bleed every month. Now you are a woman.

It's deepest winter. Cold is crawling down the mountains and into the valley. Avalanches are hanging above us. Half the village is sitting in our house. I'm serving fresh mint tea and coffee to the men. Smoking, they sit in Father's broadly striped wing chairs. Tangling men's voices and loud, deep laughter. No matter whether you like one another or not, you're thankful for the other's body heat. In winter, we huddle close together like animals in hibernation, we duck under the cold, the snow and the hugeness of the massif. It's warm and full in the kitchen, the smell of the family. The cows are kicking against the wooden wall, the heartbeat of the house. Women's voices, muffled laughter, giggling, Mother, Hülya, Esengül, Fatma and I are baking poğaça and flatbread.

I don't know where Yunus is.

Filiz!

Mister Barzan puts his hand on my shoulder.

You're smart, girl. You have to go to school in the city. Learn a profession. I'll talk to your father.

I'm climbing into the brown of the mountains. And I say the word profession, and again: profession. And then: Filiz. Filiz's profession. Profession of Filiz. Filiz-profession.

For the first time, I stroll on the way home.

I'm waiting for Mister Barzan like I wait for dawn.

I can hardly take my gaze off the hilltop over which he will have to come, Mister Barzan.

For days.

For weeks.

I'm straining milk with Mother, and there he is, standing in the stable: Mister Barzan. He wants to talk with Father.

I'm standing at the barrel without moving. The cows smell like grass and milk.

I'll betray them, the cows, I'll betray them and leave them. The stable and the whole family.

No!

Father's no rings through the walls. It is hard as stone.

Hah! At dinner, Father bursts out laughing.

He tells the story of how he sent my oldest sister to school in the city. She was supposed to become a teacher for reading and writing. To have a profession, earn money. She wanted that. And so did he.

My father already saw the envelope lying on the kitchen table, filled with liras, a monthly financial aid in old age.

My sister was living with relatives and dragged potatoes into the city by the pound, and the brothers brought her fresh yogurt and eggs, and still she regularly asked Father for money in her letters.

Father sold a cow to the neighbour or gave away a sheep, cheap, too cheap, because it had to be fast, the penniless daughter in the big city had to be fed, kept alive in the city, a question of love and honour.

My sister was smart and hardworking and finished her degree.

Then she met her future husband. She got married and had four children, and since then she bakes flatbread and gömme in the stone oven and baklava on Saturdays. She has never stood in front of a student. She has never earned a lira.

An envelope for Father never arrived.

Father says that Mister Barzan wants me to go to the city to learn a profession because he believes that I

35

am intelligent, Mister Barzan does, very intelligent, and that a profession is a necessity for my future life, for my prospective, better life, such a necessity that he offered to let me live with his relatives.

I look at Father, he nods at Mother, she ladles green-bean soup onto his plate.

Mister Barzan would take on all responsibility for me, Father says, including all costs, and that he had refused him.

His family doesn't need anyone's support.

He doesn't need this help, my father says and eats his soup.

It's a question of honour.

My world is a long, narrow hallway from which count-less doors go off left and right, hideouts, wooden dens, big, opulently decorated double doors, doors made of sandstone, of granite, doors with carvings, painted and unpainted, brown, red, black, gateways to mosques, cel-lar doors, barn doors, house entrances, I want to open them, see and enter the rooms behind them, but the doors are locked. I knock, but there's no answer. I press the door handle, jiggle it, nothing moves. I hear foot-steps, I turn around and ask strangers for the key, but they don't give it to me because they don't have it, because they know nothing about it or because they don't want me to enter a room that is strange even to them, that could mean danger to me, or strength. So I stay on the corridor. They say, get ready for the night and forget about the doors, and I become tired and for-get what a door is, what a keyhole is and what a door handle is, and so the doors become a wall.

I lie still and breathe quietly.

At night, fear seeps into the corridor, flows through the walls, through the non-existent keyholes and the cracks under the non-existent doors, like water into a leaky ship, fills the corridor, rises up to my neck. I can't put my head through the wall.

Aliye, Hüseyin and I are drinking mint tea when the doorbell rings. Aliye gets up, goes into the hallway and opens the door.

Yunus!

Her voice hurls the name into the room. A moment later: Yunus.

He has come straight from Germany after three years that he spent there. He brought the country along with him, just like that, wears Germany on his lapel, it lends shine to his hair and makes his gaze manly.

Yunus is here! Yunus! I stutter a greeting, Aliye sends me away, into the kitchen, to make coffee.

I open the cupboard and close it again, open the next, open and close, open and close, don't know where the cups are, the pot, where spoons, sugar, coffee are. I'm dumb like a sheep.

Aliye joins me in the kitchen.

What are you doing?

I don't know, I don't know.

She laughs. She puts the pot in my hand, I stand shaking, she takes it off me, makes coffee, I wash my face with cold water, drink, take a breath, we go back to the room together.

Yunus is talking to Yussuf. His black hair falls in waves, his brown eyes shine, his lips are full, his hands manicured, his shoulders are broad, on his chest I want to lie down.

He is wearing a jacket that speaks of Germany and dark blue jeans. New white trainers with red stripes.

My feet are in homemade crochet socks and brown plastic sandals. I'm wearing the flowery skirt and the old blouse.

But I'm beautiful.

I have a young, slim body, a shiny black, thick braid and big brown eyes like a cow. They shine like stars, they say. I have long, dark eyelashes, thick eyebrows, full lips and healthy teeth.

I deserve men's feet in white trainers.

I'm worth a man in jeans.

Yunus and I hardly exchange a word. What should we say and how?

Then we're alone in the kitchen for a moment.

I want you.

He is desire. Pure will.

How do we want to live, Yunus?

In jeans. We'll be wearing blue jeans. In Germany.

When Yunus leaves, he brushes against my hand as if by accident, burning cheeks and a small envelope are what remain.

I slip it under the carpet.

When I'm finally alone, I take it out, steal myself away into the chamber and open it with trembling hands.

Yunus is looking at me.

The photo has been glued into a heart-shaped paper frame.

To Filiz.

Underneath it, a purple flower blossoms.

You have to open the button on a pair of jeans, a copper- or silver-coloured one, you have to pull down the zipper, spread the opening for the hips with both hands, stand on one leg like a stork and put the other one into the trouser leg, you have to point the toes so that the foot becomes small and can find all the way through the long trouser leg until the toes reach the light on the other side of the blue tunnel and the foot finally stands on new ground, then bend the other leg, point the toes, put the foot that has become smaller through the second blue tunnel and onto the ground, the first step into a new life.

No, my father says, no.

I do not have a daughter for Yunus!

Yunus' family leaves the house without a goodbye.

I hike to the holy tree. Without Yıldız, without Aylin. Yunus in my head and in my chest. Yunus before my eyes. His breath on my tongue.

Underneath the holy tree, I kneel.

Please, holy tree, make me his wife!

I stand on tiptoe and hang a red piece of cloth into the bare branches.

Yunus and Filiz.

Snow lies on the roof tops like baked egg whites.

No stars. No moon.

The wolves' hunger grows daily. At night, they come creeping. The yellow light falling from the kitchen window is reflected in their eyes.

I don't eat and I don't drink anything. No room in my head for bread. No room for water. Heart, stomach, head, soul full of Yunus.

My mother pushes a plate of beans in front of my chest, tea.

I pick at it.

Eat!

I can't.

Eat!

She snatches the beans out from under my fork.

Hüseyin, Mehmet and Ali exchange looks. I don't catch them. I don't want to read them, eyes full of Yunus.

Filiz!

Father's voice. I'm supposed to put more wood on the fire in the bedroom oven.

I get up, wrap myself in a coat, hat and fur gloves, walk through the ice to the shed. You become quicker in the ice, you outrun time, because time freezes on your cheeks. The walk to the shed is short, too short to freeze. I come back laden with wood and go into the bedroom. I push the log into the fire, behind me:

Yunus.

We're leaving! Now! In secret!

I can't!

Come with me, else I'll leave on my own.

In my mind, I see Yunus alone in the dark, wolf eyes.

Yunus leaves.

Now Yıldız is standing in front of me.

If you love him, you have to go!

I grab a pillowcase and start cramming clothes into it at random.

Selin is standing behind me, pools in her eyes: Are you leaving?

I nod.

Selin swallows her sobs, it makes her small body swell.

Yıldız puts bread in my pillow, a bottle of water.

The dogs! We've forgotten about the dogs!

Yıldız promises to keep the dogs silent.

The house is warm, I can hear the whacking of the oven door, the creaking stairs, this is my stable. I hear laughter, my herd.

Yıldız runs to fetch Yunus.

Now he will come, up the stairs, Yunus, my future. He will take me, he will be my owner, at once shepherd and ram.

When he arrives, he grins at me. I don't know this grin.

Yıldız hands me my coat, my hat, Selin's gloves, my boots, silently I get dressed. The gloves are too small, I can't grip anything, it's too late to get bigger ones, we have to get down the stairs. In a whisper, I ask the steps not to creak. Father's voice coming from inside the room. Laughter. Pots clattering. The cows beating against the wooden wall. Where does sin begin? At the doorstep? Or at the fence?

I'm holding my breath. With the first step into the snow I am homeless.

The path that is too short for you to freeze to death ends behind the shed. The snow is deep there, sticky like honey. We sink in up to the knee, and nobody is thinking of baked egg whites any more. Yunus has become thin on the first few metres, quiet. The gate in the fence can't be opened, the snow is too heavy, we try to climb it, tearing our coats on the barbed wire. Fear is waiting on the other side, it has known about my escape longer than I have. Now there's three of us. Yunus and myself, and fear. It's a three-hour walk to

Yunus' village. During the day and in summer. Yunus offers his hand, it's hard and cold. I ask it where we're going and it doesn't know and gropes through the dark with me. Then I see a shadow: the holy tree. I've never seen it this black. I tear myself away from the cold hand, rush through the snow, toward the holy tree, kiss its frozen bark, ask for an angel so that I'll be happy.

I know Father to be raging by now, the pistol in his hand loaded, charging into the dark without a coat and barefoot. I see Father aiming at Yunus with out-stretched arms. I'm afraid he's behind us.

I hear his curses:

Your tears shall never dry!

You shall never be happy!

And I hear him crying.

For a moment, my knees weaken.

I am no longer his daughter.

Filiz! Yunus call for me with a strained voice, ducked into the darkness like a dog, fear at his hand. We have no choice. We share the night with the wolves. We fight our way through the snow. Our breath clings to the darkness like sheep's wool. So we breathe our-selves towards morning.

❀

Father's cheeks are red as apples and the veins on his forehead are blue as plums.

I have kicked his head into the dust with my ever-cold girl's feet. The barrel of the gun in his waistband is as comforting to him as the heavy, frozen wood in his hand, and Mother's barely audible screams bring him relief.

In the shed, Mother has grown stiff from the cold, the traces of tears frozen on her cheeks, her blue jewellery will be coated winterwhite soon, and the billowing breath from her mouth is delicate and fragile.

I know it.

The next day arrives without trust.

Nothing gives me shelter. Everything is exposing me. The wide, bright morning sky. The endless field of snow. The winter wind.

I am no longer a part of anything. Nothing belongs to me any more. I belong to Yunus.

I search in Yunus' eyes that don't see me, that flee from me like stray dogs. I look for an end in his hands, my end, and I fall through his fingers into the bottomless snow.

Yunus' relatives take us in. While Yunus shares a bed with the only son, I sleep in the chamber with the six daughters. The six girls are beautiful like princesses. Their long hair flows over their dresses. Their blue jewellery is dainty. Excitedly, they ask me about Yunus, envying my love, giggling, pressing me to tell them, and I too giggle and my cheeks turn red and I tell them. About the stream, about the green in Yunus' hair and eyelashes, about the radiant birthmark above his eyelid, about his big feet and his firm step.

He grabbed me like he would the mane of a foal, gripped my hair, lead me home, his foal to the shed.

The girls giggle, red spots on their cheeks.

The next day, the red spots have disappeared. As has the giggling.

I don't know where Yunus is.

The sky is grey. Everything loses its colour, its taste, its smell, its sound.

No trace of Yunus.

I long for Mother. For Father. For Yıldız, Aliye, Sayit and Selin.

I don't know where Yunus is.

The grey in my head is like the sky above the farm.

The man of the house, Yunus' uncle, slips on his fur coat, I see him tie his boots and step into the courtyard, he is going to walk through the snow and the ice to Father, ask for peace, for his consent to the marriage, for his blessing.

He looks like a crow, the man of the house, black in the white field of snow. I follow him with my eyes while the sun is rising. I can't believe that the white has an end nor the cold, that Father is living somewhere or that Mother is standing at the stove or that Selin is brushing her hair and Sayit is laughing.

I wait all day and all night.

There's nothing that can be expected of me.

She is no longer my daughter.

No blessing from me.

At night, I listen to the princesses' breathing.

I lie on my bed, knees pulled up to my chest, feet snuggled against each other, the thumbs snug in my fists as though I could take myself under my wings.

I will have a husband and lose a father. Father!

I will be married without Mother.

Without the brothers. Without my sisters.

Who will give me nuts?

Who will dance around me in a circle?

Who will sing my goodbye song?

I'm woken up by a hand on my shoulder. Yunus' mother.

I get up and stretch out my hand in order to greet her, and she places a headscarf in it.

You are going to be a wife.

She sweeps the last remaining hair off my forehead, hides it beneath the brown scarf, ties a knot, tightly underneath the chin. From the bag, she then pulls a dress, like the ones grandmothers wear.

When Yunus comes to greet his mother, he doesn't recognize me.

Yunus!

He laughs. Oh well, he says, it's only until the wedding.

Since the early hours of the morning, people I don't know have been arriving at the house. My wedding is their celebration. Their reason to laugh, to drink.

I'm quiet, a pale occasion.

Everything is lively, except for me. Everything wants the intoxication, the drunkenness, the laughter. I float like the pieces of cloth on the holy tree, which are now fluttering in the cold, heavy with rain among the bare, black branches, carrying a wish they have long since forgotten.

Like a cat, I sneak up and down the stairs.

The house smells of mint tea, the men of liquor. Waves of laughter are sloshing over the stairs.

I don't know where Yunus is.

That's when the girls come towards me, take me with them into the chamber. They have brought me a dress made from white, pressed silk and pull it over my head, it's too long. I stumble with every step, even if I stretch and walk on tiptoe, the sleeves are too long as well. I see myself in the mirror and have no more hands.

The girls excavate them from the fabric and put white gloves on them.

They place a veil on my head.

Now I'm a bride.

The girls empty their make-up bags onto the table. Mascara, lipstick, rouge, things I have never seen before.

They pluck their eyebrows, wear perfume and eye-shadow.

My eyebrows are as thick as a dog's, my hair is unkempt like a horse's tail, I have never had it cut. The only mirror is occupied by the girls. Without a mirror, I apply dark red lipstick to my lips and rouge to my cheeks for the first time.

I'm a clown.

The girls sit me down on a chair. They push a black plastic pot in my hand in which a violet flower blooms. There is a flash. A photo. With red pupils:

The bride.

There are two buses in front of the house.

One for Yunus, his family, and his friends.

And this one is for you.

I get on the bus. The girls get on with me.

We drive to the house in which Yunus has been living with his mother since his father's death. That's where I am going to live until we leave for the jeans in Germany.

The girls sing and clap their hands. The house is too close for their songs, and so the bus drives in a circle. Through the window I can see houses, stone walls, a red car, a shoe hanging on a bare tree. They roll by, the red car, the shoe hanging in the branches, again and again and always the same. The jaunty singing taunts my longing for Mother's lullaby. The girls beset me with their merriness. I am gripping the plastic flower pot so tightly with my hands that the earth spills from it. It falls onto my white lap, and I push the earthen lumps back into the black pot with my white hands.

The bus stops, the girls grab me by my arm and push me towards the house. The white dress drags along the dirty ground, grey spots creep up my dress.

Laughing people everywhere I look. I breathe alcohol.

Yunus' mother is standing in front of the entrance to her house. She is the widow here, I am the bride. There is a glass pane leaning in the door frame. I have to smash it with my feet, the shards are supposed to bring luck.

I kick the pane, the pane remains unscathed. Yelling. I try again. Laughter. Again, again, it doesn't break, again, again, it breaks. Luck is lying on the ground in front of me.

I walk across the shards into Yunus' house.

Clapping. Relief.

The celebration is not interested in me. Loud laughter, singing, clapping for no reason.

I don't know where Yunus is.

The girls return, they grab me by the shoulder and shove me forward, we're a snake, slithering through the party, it's a dance. I stumble forward, driven by foreign joy, foreign feet step on my wedding dress while foreign bodies push me forward. Just as I'm about to tear, my dress is torn.

I don't know where Yunus is.

They shove lokum into my mouth, smearing the sugar across my face, my mouth is unrecognizable in the dark, underneath the lipstick, behind the clouds of breath filled with alcohol.

They stand me in the middle of a circle, take me by the shoulders and spin me around. Dizziness. All faces are strange to me, except that of Yunus' mother.

Yunus' mother is now my mother.

She bends down to me and whispers: Mind your virgin tonight!

There she is again, my virgin. I can't see her, I can't touch her, the invisible, endangered virgin.

I run to one of the girls and whisper my despair into her ear during a dance and ask her how I am meant to mind my virgin during the night, and she says, your blood has to be clearly visible on the sheet.

They're all going to want to see it tomorrow, your blood!

I don't know how I'm supposed to manage that.

I have to cut the wedding cake, and after that they will lead me to the bedroom. I stare at the icing on the cake and the white rose made from marzipan, the music stops and finally Yunus is standing beside me, and Yunus' mother, who is now my mother, places a knife in Yunus' hand and my hand on top of Yunus' hand, and together we cut ourselves towards my virgin. Dessert plates with cake and marzipan roses on them are drifting all across the room, hands that end in people are stuck to their underside. Men, women and children with laughing mouths, who take their parties as they come, and who don't mind my virgin. A plate is pushed into my hands.

Yunus' mother, who is now my mother, leads me to the chamber, the door shuts behind me.

My stained wedding dress has become even bigger during this party, or else I have shrunk, it falls in waves around my feet, my knees are pressed together, my arms folded in my lap.

I stare at the big bed. The sheet is white as the marzipan roses, the heavy wooden frame is old and experienced.

Yunus bursts into the room, comes flying over the hill. Wolf! He comes towards me, rips the veil from my hair, shoves me against the wall, my dress has too many buttons, Yunus wants to open them, his fingers are trembling and his teeth are gritted, and then he loses his patience and he rips my dress, tears if off my shoulders, my breasts, my hips, and I shiver, and he tears up my brassiere, the underpants, and I stand naked before him, never touched, never-viewed girl, and he pulls down his trousers, his member standing in front of me, he carries it like a spear and he pounces on me, teeth first, I see slain sheep.

The pain is piercing and tough.

Slowly, Yunus, slowly.

Constrained moaning, trembling, hungry skeleton over my body.

There are men standing in front of the house, they smoke and wait impatiently for Yunus and the proof of his manhood.

They yell and whistle.

It's cold outside, too cold for two cigarettes.

The blood finally pours down between my legs. Yunus has slain my virgin. Dark spot on white sheet. Yunus kisses me, the lifeless, proudly on the forehead. He places the sheet into a basket that his mother, who is now my mother, has given him. Edge to edge, blood-stain facing up.

The wolves eat the sheep, they disembowel them. They rummage through the guts. Lungs, bowel, liver, spleen, heart, virgin.

Yunus walks through the party with the basket and flaunts my virgin.

I lie still and violated.

Bride me.

Blood on white wool. Blood on green meadow. Blood on white sheet.

I hear Mother's lament, about my bloodstained wool which you can never wash white again, or dye.

I long for my brothers, for Hüseyin, coming to cart away my corpse. I want to jolt in a wheelbarrow, across the meadow back into the stable.

The open wound throbs the next morning.

I go into the kitchen, Yunus' mother, who is now my mother, is sitting at the kitchen table, surrounded by neighbours, laughing women. The basket sits on the kitchen table. The women lift, one after the other, the sheet, they see the slain virgin and put banknotes into the basket.

I kiss the women's hands, and at the behest of Yunus' mother, who is now my mother, I stand at the stove in order to cook for the women.

I am supposed to make pasta. Helplessly, I stand in the kitchen, which is Yunus' mother's kitchen. Open the cupboards, which are Yunus' mother's cupboards, find a pot, which is Yunus' mother's pot, a wooden spoon, which is Yunus' mother's spoon, her pasta. I fill water into her pot, add the pasta, put the pot onto the stove. The pot becomes hot as does the water, it steams and bubbles, a big lump of dough is swimming in the centre, lumpy pasta, something is wrong. I'm not up to dealing with this household, so grow, Filiz, grow!

I empty the water onto the yard, it leaves a hole in the snow, a trace, the pasta I give to the chickens. They don't eat it. Then I'm standing at the stove again. Once more. Something needs to change. So once more and in a different way now.

I look around the table timidly. The pasta is edible.

My sleep is deep.

I get up in the dark and go to the stable, into the warmth of the cows, the reliable sound of their chewing, into the familiar smell. When I sit on the milking stool and draw the milk from the swollen udders, I am home. I'm looking forward to breakfast with warm flatbread and yogurt and Father and Mother, Yıldız, Sayit and Selin, I know that Father is going to appear behind me any time now, hay on the pitchfork, that he is going to wish me a good morning, Good Morning, Father!, my buckets are full and the udders empty, but I don't want to stop milking, not until Father appears behind me.

Filiz!

Yunus' mother, who is now my mother, calls for me. The flatbread on the breakfast table is warm, but without sesame and without home, I chew the bread and imagine sesame seeds between my teeth, and Mother, Yıldız and Sayit at the table and Selin on my lap.

Once I have cleared the breakfast table, I'm going to clean the kitchen and mop the floor, in the chambers too, before I'm going to boil the laundry in the yard.

Yunus doesn't work. He is the man of the house. That is enough.

Yunus is strong. He wants fresh flatbread in the mornings, which I bake for him before sunrise, fresh milk and homemade yogurt, he wants cigarettes at mid-morning, several times, with a lighter and an ashtray, for lunch he wants pilav with yogurt and turşu, in the afternoon he wants a made-up sofa to sleep on and coffee afterwards, a freshly laundered and ironed shirt, in the evening he wants washed hands, sarma and stuffed peppers, fresh cake with milk, washed feet and washed armpits, my hair newly brushed and at night he wants intercourse from the front and from behind, he wants my pain silent and my moans filled with lust.

It's Friday, we got married one week ago today. I have just washed the floor in the kitchen. Yunus is lying on the sofa and calls me, I run to him.

Fresh shirt!

I get a fresh shirt from the bedroom, put it down on the sofa next to Yunus. He points at the buttons on his chest, I unbutton them, take off the old shirt, put on the new, button it up.

Jacket!

Shoes!

I giggle, Yunus, you're eighteen, not eighty!

I'm standing in the stable among the cows, in one of the empty boxes in which we milk them, hands on the iron rod. Behind me stands Yunus with the pitchfork in his hand. He beats me with the wooden shaft. The blows are muffled. The wood sounds muffled. Inside me. He hits harder and harder. When he is out of strength, he hits with the prongs of the iron fork.

Like beating a carpet.

I topple over. Hanging over the iron rod. Throw up on the concrete floor. The cows prance anxiously, crowd against the stable walls. The blows wander over my back, my neck, my head and into my face. My eyes are bloodshot, red veins in the broken white, like marble. And blind.

I'm lying in bed. I want to turn my head, but I can't.

Yunus is sitting next to me. He's crying. He must have picked me off the iron rod like laundry off the washing line, folded me together so as to be able to carry me more easily. He's kneeling beside the bed, holding my hand and self-accusations are flowing out of his mouth like a constant stream.

Why? I ask.

You must never defy your husband!

Yunus is suffering into my hand. It's blue, black underneath the nails.

I love you, Filiz! Forgive me!

Yunus' eyes are green from bathing in the stream. He's my husband.

Everything will be all right, Yunus. I'll heal.

Homesickness is lying around everywhere, in the yard in which Selin isn't playing, in the chamber that no sister enters, in the kitchen, in the hallway, in the smell of cinnamon. Homesickness hangs in the trees, it falls from the branches. With the last snow it trickles off the rooftop as though spring was coming. The whole village is homesickness. It's there to tell me how far away I am. And that I am a child and need a home. It hears me calling this house home and laughs at me.

Yunus has a van, his pride and joy, he says, his treasure. It was once a dark green like succulent grass, but now it's russet like the meadows in August. Broken shards of glass line the rear window frame like crystals, sunlight refracts on them. For days, Yunus stands in front of his bus, his head deep inside the engine compartment, hands and face smeared with oil. The motor is faulty, the seats are torn open. I offer to sew seat covers if he buys me fabric. The next day, broadly striped polyester lies in the kitchen, dark reddish blue. I think of my father's wing chairs, crawl between the broad stripes and start sewing.

I sew the whole day, sew the whole night.

The sewing machine is a miracle machine. It draws my gaze to the tip of the needle, all thoughts, all emotions gather there. The needle is stitching my soul onto the fabric as a pattern.

At dawn, I walk into the yard and cover the seats. They are like my father's wing chairs, are the home I lost. Wondrous joy flutters, forgotten wings. I bake flatbread and set the table, I'm humming, Mother's song has lain down on my lips, when he comes, I hand Yunus fresh coffee, the warm bread and the butter, sit down, with fluttering wings, sit next to him, silently, because that's how he wants me in the mornings, silent. He chews slowly, like the cows, when he has finally swallowed the last bite, I clear the table, he leaves the kitchen and walks across the yard towards the bus, I can see it clearly through the window, the dishes in my hands clatter, I hurry, my eyes fixed on Yunus I immerse the dishes in the trough, I wash up, wipe the table and the floor underneath it, can finally run to Yunus and his joy, his amazement.

The yard is empty, the van disappeared.

At night, I hear him return.

I hear Yunus coming up the stairs and pretend to be asleep.

He enters the dark room, fills it with alcohol. I hear Yunus opening the fly of his trousers, he turns me onto my back, pulls up the nightgown and pushes into me.

Days later, the neighbour's son comes over. He tiptoes around the van and admires the wing chairs.

I'm sweeping the yard with my eyes downcast and my ears open and hear Yunus saying: Mum made them.

And Yunus' mother then tells them how she did it, tells them about patterns, seams, nights of work, every detail. The neighbour's son admires the work and Yunus' mother, who is now my mother, smiles, flattered and coquettishly like a girl.

I close my ears and lower my gaze and sweep the yard.

It was my laughter that drew the spider from her hole, to the centre of the net in which I hang, in which I'm stuck, because this is my life now.

I know that it was my laughter. I have laughed too often. That was a mistake, I know, because I am a wife.

Don't laugh! She has said that often enough, the spider, who is now my mother. I mustn't laugh, mustn't open my lips, because they're evocative of my labia and those are now Yunus' property, just like my lips. I mustn't walk through the village and give away any inkling of my lips, my lips or my labia, or even the smallest speck of my body.

Every fantasy about me belongs to Yunus.

I have laughed, opened my mouth and opened the entrance to my body, unashamedly and wide and with it the entrance to my soul, because I have cast up my eyes, that's a mistake, now she is crawling towards me, the spider who is now my mother, black and fat it comes closer, circles around me and spins her net around me, spins and spins and I stand still and pretend to be dead.

The spider has spun a cocoon around me.

I look in the mirror and can't find myself. I have disappeared into a mixture of polyester and nylon.

I am a blind spot.

I sit on the bed for hours, just like a blind spot is supposed to.

I sit still, until the black of night falls.

When Yunus comes, he's drunk. He rips the spider's web from my body, throws me onto the bed.

Underneath his steady thrusts my gaze brushes back and forth over the nightshade ceiling, back and forth.

So this is what makes me a woman again.

Yunus groans, falls into a deep slumber. I lie still. Yunus on top of me, alcohol in his blood and stomach, his sharp breath is my wakeful night.

When dawn arrives, I wriggle out from underneath Yunus and put on my clothes, layer by layer, knickers, stockings, the floor-length underskirt, the floor-length overskirt, the long-sleeved blouse, the long-sleeved cardigan, over that, for the first time by myself, the non-body, the non-face.

I am a blind spot.

I lift up my chest to catch my breath again, walk down the stairs into the courtyard.

With every step I take, I push the non-body off me.

With every step, it comes back to me.

It envelops me.

I turn my head, cheek to cheek with the non-face, look outside. The world retreats from me, it doesn't know me and doesn't communicate with me, the blind spot.

When the girls from the neighbourhood come and their giggles flow into the courtyard, I cannot remain a silent shadow. The giggles reach up to my knees, and my heart beats.

I'm a child, wife that I am.

I join the giggles and hug the girls, and I laugh and show my open mouth.

Yunus is beating me.

He has to beat the child out of my bones.

The girl out of my guts.

He has to beat the wife into my brain.

The country lies underneath a hazy white. Wafts of mist, the sky, white disc, the sun. Everything is spinning, revolves around itself and around me, I reach for the brown in the whiteness, lean on the peg of the washing line, find support, draw breath.

I'm being observed. I can feel the gaze and turn around, a toothless face grins at me. Leaning on a cane, the neighbour stands at the fence and points at my stomach:

Bebek!

The contents of my stomach spill from my mouth. I squat before the puddle, begin to count the small chunks, one, two, three, four, five, six, nineteen, twenty, twenty-three chunks, again, one, two, three, four, twenty-six, twenty-six chunks, again, nine, ten, eleven. How is a blind spot supposed to give birth to life? Twelve, thirteen, fourteen chunks! How? Fifteen, sixteen, seventeen, chunks, eighteen! How am I supposed to nurse the child from blue breasts? Nineteen, twenty, twenty-one, twenty-two, twenty-three, twenty-four! I'm unable to do what the cows do, the sheep! I have no milk from healthy breasts. No herd protecting me.

The bags with fodder are lined at the wall and weigh fifty kilos each.

I grab one, carry and pull it across the stable, lean it against the other wall, go back, get the next one, carry that one now, drop it, get the third one, then a fourth and a fifth, carry the bags back and forth, arrange them differently, like stones on a game board, lift them high, pull and drag, steaming like an animal, the heaviest I drag in a circle, panting. Maize is trickling from a minuscule hole:

No child! No child!, it writes.

No child!

I lie down on the ground and pull the heaviest of the bags onto my stomach. It crushes my breath, I lift the bag as high as I can, let it drop, onto my stomach, onto my child. Again and again.

The blood stays away.

The next day. The day after that.

Again and again, I return to the stable and play my boardgame.

Draw lines of maize like a secret confession.

Throw bags onto my child, lie silently, wait for its death.

Yunus' mother, who is now my mother, lurches toward me, I was eating her out of house and home, she yells, I eat in her home and sleep in her home, and my horrible husband does too, and she works the field, while my husband, my horrible husband, sleeps at home, my husband, who drinks, gambles, gambles away her money, the money with which she feeds us, me and my horrible husband. And the unborn child.

Yunus stands in the kitchen and yells: What more do you want? I've brought you a slave!

He drags his mother outside by her hair, across the yard and onto the street and screams: Leave!

She's with the village headman, she wants to throw you out of the house, wants to have her house cleared if you don't leave, the neighbours scold.

Yunus' mother, who is now my mother and the grandmother of my unborn child.

There is money on the table. Coins, shiny silver. Wads of notes.

Yunus provided it. He wants to pacify his mother with it.

Now we are living under one roof again, Yunus, the spider and the blind spot. And an unborn child.

The money disappears as it arrived. Yunus has gambled it away. Each bite of bread that I eat is a gift from the spider.

I am too ashamed to chew. Too proud to swallow.

.

Ramadan.

My belly is big. Yunus' mother forbids us from eating.

Me and the unborn.

Not a sip of water after sunrise, not a bite of bread before sundown.

The sun is burning down on us. We are working on the field, the unborn and I, mow, rake and turn over the grass. We bring salt stones to the animals on the field, they are meant to be well-fed and healthy.

Not a sip of water after sunrise, not a bite of bread before sundown.

I envy the sheep.

The air underneath the mixture of polyester and nylon is stale. My lips are chapped, my mouth is as hollow as my stomach.

God is great! God is greater than everything else and incomparable to anything!

I attest that there is no God but God!

Not a sip of water after sunrise, not a bite of bread before sundown.

I have loved my God.

Now I want to get rid of God.

God is great! God is greater than everything else and incomparable to anything!

I attest that there is no God but God!

To be godless at last!

At home, at my parents', God and I were friends.

We ran across the field and drove the lambs. We milked the cows and searched the meadows for herbs. We enjoyed the shower of rain and the brothers' sweaty smell. We talked long and often and were silent together at night. We fought, because of the sprained ankle. We trusted one another.

Maybe he is still talking. I don't hear anything any more.

Trapped in the mixture of polyester and nylon I am deaf.

Each day feasting becomes harder, the cracks in my lips deeper.

The hunger, the hunger, hungry dog. My head hurts, in my belly the child. Its kicks become weaker. It's hot.

Drought all around us.

I'm milking the cows. I immerse my hand in the bucket, scoop by cupping my hand, the milk smells fatty and sweet, I drink like a calf. Behind me: the spider. Beating my hands, my head.

She denies milk to me and my child, in the name of God. Insults me and curses: You're godless! Godless you will be!

It's a promise to me.

The hunger, the hunger, hungry dog.

I don't fast for God.

I fast for myself. I fast so that I won't owe the spider anything.

After sundown, the opulent table: golden-baked börek, sarma, steaming pilav, deep-red turnip salad with fresh parsley, mild cacık, yayla soup with fresh peppermint, barbunya that looks the same way it did at home.

With one look, the spider locks my jaw, chokes me.

A bite of bread, a sip of water, half a spoon of barbunya. No more.

Nothing more.

Away from the table I don't eat anything either. As though the börek would inciminate me, as though the halva could betray me to the spider.

One night I force myself to eat. I have to. I'm carrying a child inside me. Under the spider's gaze I lift the fork, open my lips, eat a piece of cheese, the property of the spider that I have drawn from the cows's udders, carried to the barn, dried to cheese. I have a piece of spider-property on my tongue, it tastes salty, greasy and alien, as though I was eating the spider itself, I chew slowly and order my larynx to swallow. It's still compliant, but my stomach doesn't obey me any more.

I vomit the spider's property onto the yard.

81

Mother. Mother!

My mother is coming!

She's still far away, but she is walking towards me, I begin to run, run towards her, with fluttering wings towards her, my mother, my mother! She doesn't recognize me. She wants to pass me.

Mummy!

Uncertain, my mother looks into the blind spot, searches for her daughter in it.

Won't find it in there.

Mummy!

I want her embrace.

Mother is unable to grab the blind spot, cannot touch it.

Mummy!

Filiz?

Mother's voice is thin.

I grow and greet her in a steady voice, tell her about the joyous pregnancy and Yunus, the good husband. I soak every word in joy.

I'm well!

I ask about Father, who doesn't have a daughter any longer. About Selin. About Sayit, Yıldız, Hüseyin, about Aliye and Royin, about our cows and lambs, about the neighbours and the fields.

I'm well!

I'm drowning in joy.

Mother is struggling to believe me.

Her gaze is timid.

She leaves without a single touch.

Intercourse. Yunus is lying on top of me, his big feet sticking out over the edge of the bed, his stiff member pushing inside me. In my dreams, Yunus' member protrudes from the green water of the stream into the deep blue sky, it's warm and shiny in the sunlight, in the darkness of the bedchamber it's cold and sharp like broken glass. Yunus' body is like iron, a tarnished chest, his lips float high above mine, his eyes are invisible. He pushes into me, the blind spot. While he pushes, I silently voice my yearning towards him. Deaf, he pushes and moans loudly.

Get up!

It's still night when the spider beats against the door in order to wake me.

You're a wife, not a child!

I get up, Yunus wraps my blanket around him, I get dressed, and my unborn and I go into the stable to milk the cows.

Yunus hasn't spoken a word to me in days. No order.

I kneel down before him and beg.

His silence is as big as my fear.

At night, I dream that I enter Yunus' throat like a tunnel so as to break words from his gums. I dare to venture deep inside, but I can't recover anything. That's when the throat starts to crumble, caves in, the tongue flips, I fall into the abyss.

Free falling.

The silence is an arrangement between Yunus and the spider, I hope.

I wash Yunus' feet, every day, when he comes home, from the outside that is not due to me. I wash them with water and soap, I hold them in my hands and don't want to let them go, I talk to them, quietly, tell them about our unborn child. I dry and anoint them.

Yunus sleeps in another room now.

I go to him. I kneel down beside his bed, take off my veil, my waistcoat, my blouse, my brassiere, I hold my ample, milk-filled breast out to him, they are beautiful and white in the semi-dark, the nipples jut out bravely into the dark.

Do you want to?

Silence.

I take off my skirt, my stockings, take my underwear down over my knees, am naked, offer myself to him.

Yunus doesn't look at me.

I press my lap into his hand.

He doesn't move.

I stare at his mouth. I know that he can speak.

Say: I hate you! Please!

Silent as a stone.

I get up, grab my clothes, steal away like a mangy dog.

I long for his beatings.

In thirty-six hours, Yunus will have returned. He has driven into the city, with the neighbour's son, I don't know why. He didn't tell the spider about it, but he told her that he would return, tomorrow night, thirty-six hours later, in thirty-six hours Yunus will have returned.

I wait for him to return to me, I wait for myself to return to me with him. I wait for my return to being.

When he comes back, he turns me onto my stomach, pushes up my nightdress, grabs my arms, pushes them onto the mattress on either side of my head, pushes his member between my legs.

He leaves the room without a word. The child and I remain alone.

The child inside me moves. I sing us both to sleep.

At night, the silence weighs heavier.

Yunus enters my doze, a shadow without a mouth, without eyes, just a piece of paper. On it, written in capital latters: Calve!

The cow's calls invade my daze.

I'm jolted, get dressed and run to the stable. The cow is lying on the floor screaming, two of the calf's legs jut out from inside her.

The animals are at home here. I am a stranger. I pile the hay in front of their mouths, check the water and re-attach salt stones that have fallen to the floor, I shovel fresh straw underneath their hooves. I clean a stranger's stable, milk a stranger's cows and carry a stranger's milk. When I leave the stable with full buckets, I feel like a thief. I collect the eggs from the chicken coop, steal them as well. I prepare scrambled eggs and set the table and when Yunus arrives, everything is ready. I sit silently, as Yunus wants me to, a meal with silent company.

He chooses from the freshly baked bread that I hand him, I spread butter on it, spoon sugar in his coffee, he takes a sip.

Mother! Yunus roars.

Mother!

I hear her feet touch the floor next to the bed, hear footsteps in the chamber, steps on the stairs, she pushes the kitchen door open.

Tell Filiz that the coffee is too thin!

I clear the table, fetch water from the well, boil it and scrub the laundry. Yunus' trousers and underwear, his shirts, his socks, Yunus' mother's stockings, her blouses and undergarments, her skirts, her sheets. The water turns brown, I walk to the well, two buckets in my hand to get fresh water, that's when my child kicks me.

At noon, I cook. Lentils and cured lamb. I cut lettuce. Yunus is lying on the sofa. He is sleeping.

Lunch is as silent as breakfast. The yearning for a word from Yunus is as big as his silence. The yearning for his touch. For me. For the child.

The spider sits down at the table. She eats. I don't eat. I know that my tongue gets tied in her presence. That my gums hang low and my voicebox won't move any more, that my mouth dries out, that, I know.

Don't eat from her hand!

Everything that lies in front of me in this house comes from her hand.

Big, heavy, fat spider! Now she is sitting on the bench by the stove.

Yunus wants his jacket and shoes. Points his finger.

I put his jacket on him, kneel down, take off his slippers and put on his shoes, tie the laces into a bow, grab his feet with both hands, want to sink down to his ankles, skin for me, for the child. I don't dare to.

Yunus gets up and walks out of the house. I can hear the sound of the motor of his bus.

I clear the table, sweep the floor in the kitchen and the bedchambers, chop wood, stack a pile of wood in the shed, milk the cows, feed them. Then I prepare dinner.

The set table stands lonely and silent in the dusk. I sit and wait. Time passes.

Unmoving, I wait for Yunus until late into the night, until I am cold.

Yunus doesn't come.

I put the food back into the cupboards, I dare to, I must, I eat.

Later, Yunus comes into my chamber, he is holding a glass of water in his hand. He comes to the bed and holds the glass out to me.

It's cool and smooth and filled to the brim.

As though Yunus had brought the world to the bed for me.

I drink it in big gulps.

One morning, I place my feet in the snow. Autumn had remained unnoticed by me, I don't know whether the leaves were colouful, for how long they were handing on the trees. I don't know when it began to snow.

Yunus has been silent for one hundred and thirty-seven days.

I wish myself a good morning. I praise myself for my baklava, it turned out nicely, Filiz! I am happy about my clothes, you are a skilful seamstress, I prepare breakfast, adjust the teaspoon on Yunus' saucer and whisper, thank you, Filiz! While milking the cows, I chat to myself about Seda's broken leg that has long since healed, about Leyla's gems and the disappeared ball, I declare my love to myself while washing the floor, I love you, Filiz!, when fetching water, you are my star!

And sometimes I say: I am afraid.

The child in my belly is alien, a threat. It only kicks me and feeds off me. It's as silent from the inside as its father is from the outside.

I cover myself with words. Everything will be all right. Everything will be all right.

Even though I don't believe myself.

Everything will be all right.

I make a doll, just like I did as a young girl, from a piece of wood and bread dough, it receives raisins for eyes and hair from straw and a dress wound from a piece of cloth that I have left over from making the cushion covers, striped red and blue. With straw, I braid lips with which it can speak, paint them red for sumptuous words.

It speaks of everything and everybody, of the calves and lambs, of Mother's halva and the brothers, of the boat made from bark that sank in the puddle, and of green strawberries.

My belly is growing. The unborn child takes over my being. I am its nourishment, its breath, its instrument made from skind and bones, the legs and arms stuck to the amniotic sac.

I'm scared of the birth.

I'm at its mercy. Clueless. Alone.

Yunus' silence is the only thing I can rely on. It evaporates from his breath, permeates his gestures, it's his smell.

I will bear his child into his silence.

The monologues sprawl in my mouth like weeds, I love you, Filiz, I love you, love you, loveyouyouyou-youyouyou.

The spider is crouching behind the door, listening.

Filiz is going crazy, she says to Yunus.

Every man that comes down the frozen village street is my father for a moment. My fathers slip on the patches of ice, they trudge through the freshly fallen snow, I can make out the imprints of their feet for a long time after.

Every day, my fathers pass. Alone. With wives and children. With daughters. Sometimes they come together, in twos or threes or in a group. They carry wood together or shindles, or they sit on the horse-drawn carts and drive by without a word of greeting.

Later, much later, he comes, my father. He comes along the village road, like my mother, I can see him from afar, he approaches me, comes towards me, I stand still, not breathing, he stops right in front of me. He looks into the blind spot and searches for his daughter, wants to find her. Brave father.

My bosom is large. My belly is overwhelming. I am nothing but blemish.

Father takes me into his hard arms, his embrace is strong, it takes away my power. I cry.

Yunus is not enjoying his heavily pregnant wife.

She is no longer arousing.

I hear as he tells the spider this, my hands in the dishwater.

He wants to go away, take the bus to Kiğı or somewhere, for one or two weeks, tomorrow morning.

I take my hands out of the dishwater, kneel down before him, kiss his hand. Please be with me when I deliver our child!

A few hours later, snow starts falling again. Thick flakes, the whole night through. The clouds are still heavy at dawn. The streets are icy. No coming through. Yunus has to stay.

It snows the whole day, the whole night.

The next morning, I am awoken by pain. Pain in my belly. Pain in my back. Pain between my legs. The pain makes me go in a circle, urges me out of the chamber, out of the house.

I stand in the courtyard in my nightdress and vomit onto the frozen ground.

The spider pulls me into the house, onto a bedstead in the kitchen, in front of the oven. She yells: Yunus!

He is to fetch Hatice, because Hatice is the one who supervises births in the village.

I see Yunus come down the stairs, put on his shoes and the jacket, I pant, I see him leave the house. Not a word, no glance from him.

And suddenly I am the spectacle. The village gathers in our house. The neighbour women are standing in our kitchen, forming a circle around me.

Hatice spreads my legs and my labia. The amniotic fluid has long since dried, the birth canal dried up. They decide to take me to the hospital, through the snow.

Yunus swears and starts the bus.

I lie on the red-and-blue-striped seat covers, wrapped in blankets. The contractions come in shorter and shorter intervals. At walking pace, we drive through the flurry of snow. For hours.

The child they place on my stomach is red, smeared in blood, with big brown eyes. The skin puckers around his small body.

A son.

It's the 24th of December.

His name is Halil, Yunus says.

Stop! I want this to stop!

When the newborn screams, Yunus also screams.

I can't take this crying!

I let the child feed from my breast and leave the room. We're on the run, the child and I, always ready to jump up and run on. We flee many times a day. From room to room. From the house to the yard, from the yard to the stable, from the stable to the yard, from the yard to the house, from the stairs to the kitchen, to the bedchamber, from the chamber to the stairs, from the stairs to the kitchen, I cannot calm the child.

The spider scolds louder than ever. Now there's three people eating everything she owns.

At night, I dream that we're sitting in the yard, the newborn and I, breaking off pieces from the house and putting them into our mouths. We chew the brickwork slowly and swallow deliberately.

When Yunus isn't yelling, we live in Yunus' silence. I am sure that Yunus is never going to speak to me again, when suddenly a word falls to my feet.

Hand.

He waits for an answer.

I remain silent.

Again and again, I stumble over single words.

Son.

They are sticky and rough, but I grab them and place them underneath my blouse. There they grow and become soft and warm.

Please, silence, lift yourself! Day by day.

Yunus has been called to do his military service. His bag is lying on the bed, I'm packing his things. The spider cowers in the corner and lies in wait. Until Yunus returns, I will be living in the centre of her web, for eighteen months.

A car horn rings out in the yard.

A car is parked in front of the house. Two men get out. They have come to fetch Yunus, bring him to the army that needs him.

I counted five hundred and forty-four days. I have been the spider's slave for five hundred and forty-four days. Halil is not allowed to sleep in my bed any longer. He is not allowed to call me Mummy any more. He now calls the spider Mummy and calls me Auntie. Halil belongs to the spider now. I have stopped eating.

I am a piece of dirt.

Yunus is going to be back in seven days.

The day is overcast. A dark green car drives onto the yard, a man gets out, a soldier. He walks across the yard, knocks on the door. The spider opens. I stand in the hallway and listen.

Yunus' service is prolonged as a punishment. He is going to return two months later than expected.

Yunus is lying dead in the mountains. His legs are twisted. They carried him, by his hands and feet, threw him into the grass. Flies crawl into his chest through the wound. Yunus is staring into the blue sky. He's well camouflaged in his uniform, is a patch of grass with dead eyes and heavy boots.

Yunus is walking towards the house, the bag thrown over his shoulder, his hair cropped. My heart stops beating. He sees me through the window. I don't breathe. He pushes open the door, lets his bag fall to the ground, embraces me, holds me, his hand lies on my hair, his mouth on my neck, his breath moves my chest, my heart begins beating again. I am happy.

Soon my belly begins to grow again.

I'm standing at the stove, two scarves covering my hair, my forehead, my temples, the blouse fastened to the chin, flowing to the knuckles, two floor-length skirts. There's a knock. As though there were an outside, something beyond the house, as though the spider's house wasn't the world. I open, head bowed, gaze lowered, the village hodja is standing on the doorstep, a servant of God, a friend of the spider. He is evil, for he is sacred to the spider. Head bowed, gaze lowered and in a muffled voice I answer his questions.

My husband is asleep. His mother is not here.

With downcast eyes, I nod a goodbye and the door closes as Yunus' flat hand slaps my head off my neck.

Yunus drags me across the stone floor in the yard and into the stable. He fetches a rope, places it around my neck. The knot doesn't turn out the way he wants it to for long time. He swears. I keep still.

Stand on the stool!

I stand on the stool.

Put your hands behind your back!

I put my hands behind my back.

He binds them, the wire cutting into my wrists, the fingers swelling. Yunus fastens the rope around my neck to the wooden beam above me.

I think of the unborn child in my belly. Its body is light, but its soul is heavy.

Yunus is crying.

You dare to speak to a man?

He kicks the stool out from under my feet.

I am hanging from the beam, Yunus leaves the stable.

I flutter, wire around my wings, draw blackness in through the pupils.

No light. No God as once promised.

I die from Yunus' hand.

So that was the meaning of me.

Then the black wave arrives.

It's the spider who enters the stable just in time.

Father is coming! Father! He's come to take me home, as though I were his daughter.

When he comes closer, I see: Father has become old from the fate that I am. He is tired, withered grass for which there is no more spring.

We walk across the mountains. I smile.

Mother and the brothers nod a greeting. I listen to the brothers' laughter, but I don't hear it. There's no word leaving the sisters' mouths. I reach for Mother's hand. It's cold.

I'm in my home that is my home no longer, that had always been my rescue in need and doesn't rescue me from my misery now.

One evening, I look through the window of the chamber, Yunus and the spider are standing in the dusk. Something is happening. No sound reaches me, I can't read their gestures.

Yunus storms inside, he yells: We're leaving!

His scream is like a shot.

The evening sky, the yard, the house, our life shattered, the shards are lying scattered.

We rumble across the countryside in the bus, the house has descended behind the hill.

The street dust sticks Halil's eyelashes together, at last, he closes his eyes, I don't have to bear his gaze any longer.

The hilly countryside is behind us, darkness dominates the inside of the bus, then it creeps across the fields, the plain is black. Are we going to Germany now?

We're standing in Elazığ, in front of Yunus' cousin's door, one child by the hand, another in the belly. The cousin's loaf of bread is big, but not big enough, and his gyros isn't enough for his four children, his wife and us.

I feed Halil and stay hungry.

At night, the three of us are lying on a mattress.

During the day, I keep stealing away to the bathroom and lock myself in, I dance with my fingers on the white tiles.

Seven days.

Often, I take Halil with me. Quietly he sits on the tiled floor.

I try to help Yunus' cousin's wife, we can't wash the floors, there are children everywhere, clothes, blankets. The guilty conscience is dancing on the white tiles in the bathroom. The four children romp and scream, Halil stands in the way shyly. Yunus sits in the only armchair. Yunus' cousin leaves for work at four-thirty, in order to bring home meat and bread.

My contractions set in. I look at the white tablecloth and the light-coloured sofa and don't dare having the child.

At the hospital, I hold my girl in my arms. Selin. She's delicate.

I am her mother. This time I am the mother.

The door opens and Yunus enters with flowers, yellow roses, wrapped in cellophane. The smell remains wrapped in the foil. For the nurse, Yunus brought chocolates.

The next day we're sitting in the bus again, Selin in my arms, Halil leaning against my shoulder.

Elazığ's streets are in uproar, they rise up and bow down and throw the whole country into chaos, today is the anniversary of Atatürk's death, screams and yelling, buses and rusty cars sounding their horns.

Atatürk is long dead, our daughter has just been born.

She will be smart like Atatürk, Yunus says as he unlocks a front door.

We enter a huge, empty flat, floor, ceiling, walls of concrete. The November cold hangs between the walls. The newborn in my arm and Halil on my hand I walk through the long hallway, rooms left and right, empty, only one room has a carpet in it, blue, as though a piece of sky had fallen to the floor. Yunus sets down a plastic bag in front of me, in it a trussed chicken, eggs, milk, flour, onions, a bag of coal.

I will be gone often and for long periods of time.

He leaves. The door shuts behind him, I hear him turning the key, three times, we're locked in.

Grey clouds flow into the grey rooms. The children are as quiet as I am. There's an oven in one of the rooms, a water pipe protrudes from the wall, an aluminium sink underneath it. I heat up the oven, prepare a bedstead for the children from clothing and without a pan I fry the cold chicken. Then night comes. Above us men's voices, underneath us booming music. The walls are as thin as we are. It's only when the men's voices fade, the music ends, that we find sleep.

I wake up because the key is turning in the lock. Yunus has brought blankets, a pot, a big knife and cutlery, diapers for Selin and washing powder. A chicken, potatoes, rice, peppers, garlic, butter and salt.

First, I cook the chicken in the only pot, then the rice.

Yunus kisses his daughter, takes her into his arms and lies down with her on the bedstead, his hand on the small cheek, fingers in the tufts of hair. Yunus rocks Selin.

He reaches out his hand to Halil, come!

Halil shivers, he presses himself against the wall.

Come!

Halil doesn't move.

Come, Halil!

Halil approaches Yunus, fingers balled into fists, toes curled. Step by step he balances towards his father, white as chalk. Brave boy, brave Halil. Yunus pulls him down to the floor with him.

Trembling, Halil lies in Yunus' arms.

After dinner, Yunus goes into the bathroom with me. He stands me up against the wall, pulls up my skirt, we have to be quick.

Then the door falls shut. The key turns. Three times.

I don't know when the next chicken will arrive.

We wait for the sound of the key in the lock.

I hear it in my dreams. When I am awake. The key seems to turn for days. It unlocks our ears and locks our heads.

Then they are here. Yunus and the chicken. Out of the blue.

There's fresh flatbread, apples and pears, cucumbers, tomatoes, pepper and paprika powder, ayran and yogurt and fresh milk.

Yunus eats, sleeps, pushes inside me, and leaves.

We're alone again.

Mummy, Halil says and means me.

Yunus has brought a man with him, Ali, his wife Sahime and their two children.

They are going to live here.

He sets down bags in the room, pushes inside me quietly in the bathroom, the door falls shut, the key turns.

Ali has gone as well. Sahime cries silently. She's adorned with blue, wearing a medallion around her neck. She pulls up the collar of her cardigan, I turn away. Blue jewellery is private property.

Soon Sahime's eyes begin to reflect concrete as well. We look at each other and become walls. We only shift ourselves slowly. From the bedstead to the bathroom, to the kitchen, back onto the bedstead.

Time has stopped running through our fingers.

The children have stopped growing.

The men are standing in the hallway, they are black silhouettes, their skin smells of sun.

They find holes in the walls that we are and stick their dicks into them.

They caress the children's hair.

They throw a chicken onto the stove.

When Yunus beats me, I know that Sahime hears us. Every blow makes her blue jewellery tremble, her necklace sounds bright and her bracelets jingle, Sahime stirs something in the pot on the stove. When I return to the kitchen, I'm grateful that she averts her gaze. Blue jewellery is private property.

A few days later, my blue jewellery is trembling, I hear Ali's beating, stir the pot and know of Sahime's blue arms, her blue belly, her blue back, her blue legs.

It's only when the door shuts behind the men the next morning that I dare go to her. Sahime has pulled the covers up to her chin. Her mouth is sealed shut.

The men are gone for a long time. Weeks. Maybe months. A neighbour unlocks the door, puts food into the hallway, locks the door again.

The time without beatings is paradise. Space for our heartbeat.

Pack our things!

Yunus has come out of the blue, is standing in the hallway now.

We're leaving!

The spider laughs out loud when we drive into the courtyard.

She has grown in our absence, has grown taller than my head. I have shrunk. I won't be able to live in her shadow any longer, Yunus!

When Yunus drags me from the car, she looks without shame into my face that I want to hide beneath the headscarf.

What kind of a pest bird are you bringing into my house!

Halil sits behind the window and doesn't move.

Yunus drags him from the car as well.

The spider runs her fingers through Halil's hair.

Silently we slip into the past and forget the future.

Yunus disappears.

Halil starts calling the spider Mummy again.

More and more frequently, my knees break, my body crumbles.

I lie motionless until the spider comes and beats me to my legs.

I hear the neighbour women whisper. The lean down to me and whisper the song of the blue women into my ear.

This is your fate, you have to live this way, even if he is a dog.

We have to live this way, we have to suffer this way, we can't help ourselves.

Think of the children!

At night, the wind whistles the song of the blue women around the house.

And the witch living next to us hisses over the fence, drink the water in which you have washed your mother-in-law's feet.

It's her bed you're sleeping in, her farm, her water, her bread that feeds you and your family.

Yunus has gone to Austria. Not to Germany. To see his uncle. He wants to look for work and fetch us later, to Europe.

The sun rises in the West.

Austria is a land of the rising sun. The land of jeans and sneakers. There are jeans that are tight at the top and become wider at the calves, there are jeans that are loose on the hips, they hang so low that the crack between the cheeks becomes visible when you bend over. There are dark jeans, there are light-coloured ones and there are some that look as though they're washed out even though they are new, you can buy them with small spots or with large ones, there are jeans whose hem is already frayed when you buy them, there are also jeans that you buy with big tears at the knees. Then the pockets. There are those sewn in at the sides and those sewed on at the hip, small, narrow ones into which you can barely stick a finger, and big ones that fit the whole hand, some have a flap and a button. Everyone in Austria wears jeans. Everyone can have jeans there, everyone can wear them, men and women. And then the sneakers: made from smooth leather or full-grain leather, with Velcro, with laces, with one, two, or three stripes, in white or green, in yellow, blue or pink, as though jeans and sneakers grew on the fields there, lush like weeds.

Austria is like Germany. Austria may be smaller, but it has the same jeans with the same sewn-on pockets and the same buttons, it has the same sneakers, and on the sneakers, there are the same red stripes, if not more. Austria and Germany are countries like life on television, without poverty and illness, and the supermarkets are stuffed with colourfully wrapped delicacies from all over the world. Austria is like Germany, and Germany is like America. And that's where the sun rises.

Yunus can't find work.

He writes that the only way of getting the children and me to Austria is by marrying an Austrian woman.

The spider shows me the letter. Yunus' handwriting is still as beautiful as on the heart-shaped picture frame made from paper. I read and nod.

Jeans and sneakers are going to enter Yunus' life on the legs of another woman.

Time grows weaker and weaker. Every day, it's supposed to give birth to another day. Every night another night. And every hour another hour. Seconds every second. Time has become tired. More and more often than before it sits in the courtyard, next to the cold wall, quiet and without being. And I milk the cows for ever, and the walk to the well has no end.

But Yunus doesn't marry.

Mummy, I'm hungry!

I scrub the stains off the kitchen floor, the stains, the stains.

Mummy, I'm hungry!

I look up at Halil, his eyes are big, behind them are Selin's hungry eyes.

I rise, go to the pantry, my steps are small. I steal cheese and bread. I'm brave enough to warm milk. I feed the spider's scolding to the children, spoon humiliation into their mouths, thin, they run back to the yard before they are full.

I kneel on the kitchen floor, plunge the brush deep into the bucket. I stop breathing, my body falls heavy onto the tiles.

In my lack of power, I run across the street, across the fields, reach the trees, hide in the thicket like an animal.

I breathe. In. Out.

My fear rustles in the branches. It grows in the form of grass underneath my feet. In the form of a branch it hits me in the face. I have nothing but my veils and the bones underneath them, black, dried-out hair and lips, pale and bitten, meagre eyes, everything hidden in black. The fear of disappearing within myself grows in my head, I want to go on, want to flee, but my feet are silent. That's when the fear blossoms silvery, and my fate of disappearing within myself becomes salvation.

Why not?

I'm lying in a white bed and am getting my heartbeat back, and my thoughts.

My ovaries are inflamed and reach up to my throat.

Yunus is sitting at my bed.

I have seen many husbands, the nurse whispers to me, but none has cared for his wife as lovingly as yours! Her round schoolgirl eye winks at me. He flew in from Austria for you!

Yunus brings me flowers that don't smell, and chocolates without a taste. Nothing he puts into my hands, or onto my tongue, or in my line of sight tastes, smells, or talks.

How lovely they smell! the schoolgirl says and puts the flowers in a vase.

Yunus stays by my bed.

That evening, the ovaries grow out of my throat.

I heave up every sip of water.

Yunus is leaning over me like he does over the motor of his bus.

I need you, says Yunus, I love you, once you're well again, we'll leave this place.

I'm standing on the doorstep next to my husband, the suitcases are packed, our faces are turned towards the distance. No word of farewell to the spider, no touch.

I agree with Yunus.

Twenty-four hours on the bus, the children on our laps, take us away.

Istanbul is a bungalow. Made from concrete like the flat in Elazığ, but small and at ground level.

Istanbul is by the sea. We cannot see it, but since the concrete is fresh and still wet, we live with the tide. At night, the water rises from the floor, puddles spread. In the mornings, the water reflects the greyness, one of our things or another here and there: an empty sardine tin, a plastic bag. Like storks the children stalk around the bungalow, they cast for the plastic bag and play with it. I mop the floor dry, take the carpet off the hook in the ceiling and put it back on the floor. I boil potatoes and do the laundry.

Yunus is gone often and for long periods of time, my blue jewellery wanes. At night, I put the carpet on the hook and we sleep. I have the children in my arms, the mattress stays damp. When I wake up at night, I see the water rising from the floor again.

We still live without beatings.

Pink flowers blossom on the pile of rubbish behind the house.

Yunus is gone for a long time. Our shoulders sink. Without beatings we blossom, the children and I.

My thoughts dare to venture from the backyards. I'm standing on the street in front of the house, and the wind blows the sea into my face. My skin becomes salty and my chest wide. I breathe deep and let the headscarf slide into my neck for a moment.

Zarife, the neighbour, smiles at me, she opens her headscarf and copies me.

She's from Tekbaş, just like I am. She has run across the fields of my childhood, she knows the taste of barely ripe pears hanging in the wind in early autumn, has grown up with them and longs for them, just like I do.

Zarife!

We want to become friends and tell each other more.

Zarife!

I'm coming!

Hastily, she ties up her headscarf and disappears inside the house.

Yunus sends money for food.

Round, hard coins that I could turn into meat. But I scrimp and save up for a home. I boil potatoes and rice instead of meat and buy a table.

I give the children water instead of milk and sew cushions and tablecloths, no spices, no honey, I hang curtains in front of the windows. I can finally buy a pan, glasses, plates. At the bazaar, I find a wooden doll on invisible strings, for the first time, the children have a toy.

Yunus comes.

Yunus pushes inside me.

Yunus gets me with child.

Bebek!

Yunus puts money on the table. Coins, notes.

I have never seen this much money.

What am I to do with the money, he asks, have you gotten rid of the child or bought a fridge?

Get rid of the child, I say, please!

The new fridge is shiny and white and hums, a small, blue light flashes even at night.

I think of the child inside me, growing incessantly.

Onion steam gets rid of unborn children, Zarife says, you have to squat over the steaming pot with your legs spread.

I buy three kilos of fresh onions, squat with spread legs, onion tears roll across my cheeks. The child stays.

If you take a lot of pills, doesn't matter which, unborn children disappear, the woman at the bazaar says.

I take pills against the flu, pills against fever, against headaches and joint pains, against bronchitis and stomach pains, I take five of each. Nothing happens.

The child stays.

It will probably come in autumn.

One morning, blows fall from the sky, unexpected and icy, like snow in August.

I'm lying on the floor and wait for movement from the unborn child.

It floats in the amniotic fluid, in the swooshing without a heartbeat. Yunus is flailing at me. At my arms, my chest, my belly, at the unborn child.

I'm standing between display cases full of gold. Earrings, bracelets, necklaces, rings. Pink letters stuck to the display window: Clearance sale!

Yunus points at a necklace with a golden heart. The jeweller opens the display case, picks the necklace from the plastic neck and hands it to Yunus. Yunus places it around my neck and smiles, the jeweller nods.

Jewellery. Gold and blue.

Dawn. The child is pressing against my pubic bone. I get up and bake bread.

Yunus chews evenly, after the last bite he takes his jacket.

Don't go, Yunus, please!

Yunus lurks.

The child is coming! I promise in a brittle voice.

Yunus lights a cigarette, he takes a deep drag, calls his will off the street like a mutt.

He sits back down at the table, stares into my face, at my belly.

Selin and Halil have stopped chewing the bread in their mouths.

Above all, the alarm clock is ticking. At the end of time lies the child or blue jewellery.

Amid the loud ticking the unborn child remains motionless.

The next morning, I awake clad in new blue jewellery. The amniotic fluid is running down my legs, this time I don't dare to ask for help.

I bake bread and make coffee and hand Yunus his jacket, he leaves.

The contractions force me to my knees and then onto all fours, like a cow. Halil stares between my legs, Selin squats before me, Mummy!

The neighbours come and scream and push and pull at me. I scream like a cow.

The child is stuck.

In the taxi to the hospital I bite my lips bloody, only dripping blood, caught in the rear-view mirror, no sound from the man at the steering wheel.

With the aid of the ventouse, they drag to light the one who doesn't want to be born.

It's a girl, Seda, squashed and ugly, blazoned with blue jewellery from the beginning.

I have no milk in my breasts for the newborn.

A photo of my new happiness?

I hide the girl from the hospital photographer underneath the blanket.

The next morning, Yunus takes us back to the bungalow.

Zarife is waiting there with Selin and Halil and a bouquet of pink flowers in her hand. I'm tired. I hug Zarife and the children and lie down on the damp mattress with the newborn girl.

When I wake, Yunus' cousins are sitting at our table. Their hands rest on Halil's shoulder. They take Halil to the village. In spring, they are going to circumcise him.

I pack Halil's bag. Halil is pale.

I put Halil's jacket on him. Silently, he follows the men. Seda has come, Halil leaves. I don't want a new child.

I want Halil.

Halil!

Filiz! Filiz! Screams outside the house. Children's screams.

Selin is screaming!

The door is pushed open, Zarife is standing there, Selin in her arms. It was a game! Zarife's daughter is crying, it was a game!

While playing, Selin fell off the wall.

She can't stand up any more!

I stand her on the floor, she slumps down like a house of cards. I lift her up, stand her on her legs again, carefully.

She can't stand up!

Yunus is going to beat me to death.

Selin's hip is fractured.

My child is broken.

Selin lies small on the big hospital bed on wheels, the glass door closes behind her, the doctors are white shadows.

Yunus is going to beat me to death.

Here's the bill, Mrs Şahin.

Yunus is going to beat me to death.

Hours later, a nurse hands me my child, in a cast from head to toe.

Come back in six weeks.

Selin is as stiff as her cast. Silent as her cast. Heavy as a stone. I can barely carry her.

I'm sitting on the bus, my child in her cast in my arms.

Yunus is going to beat me to death.

Yunus adorns me with blue, blue bodice, blue stockings, a choker. Blue rings on my fingers. He beats a tiara onto my forehead.

Outside the cast, and inside the child. It screams the whole night through.

Four weeks later, Yunus takes a knife and cuts the child from the cast. Selin emerges slowly, white and fragile like a sculpture. I stand her on her legs, and she walks towards me, shaking.

Yunus sends us back to the village.

The heat on the bus is unbearable, as is the smell. Drunk men behind and in front of me, next to me a woman with a chicken on her lap. I sit squashed, in each arm a child that can't sleep. The window rattles. I don't dare to look at the men's faces. For twelve hours, my head and eyes remain bowed. The arms around the girls clenched.

At the rest stop, everyone rushes from the bus, only I remain sitting, the girls in my arms, we play dead.

The drunk men come back even drunker, the chicken sits down next to me, we drive on, towards the spider.

Suddenly: next stop!

I grab the girls, jump up and drag the suitcase into the dust.

The bus disappears, the dust settles, we're alone. I'm sitting on the ground, next to the suitcase, the sleeping girls still in my arms, then night comes.

There's no bus to Bağlar until the morning. I wake up Seda and Selin, and with the sleepy girls I get onto the bus that is going to take us to the spider. Halil is living by the spider's side. My Halil. Finally, I am going to see Halil again.

Halil cowers in the centre of the web shyly, he has grown, I run towards him, he clenches his fists inside his trouser pockets. It's days before he lets me take him in my arms and cries.

In spring, Yunus finally sends the documents we need in order to enter Austria.

Sinner! Sinner!

The spider ambushes me. You want to live in Austria? With infidels! Everything you eat there is sin! The meat in Austria is sin. The carrots. The courgettes. The tomatoes. Each spoon of yogurt is a spoon full of sin. Every sip of milk is a sip of sin. Every bite of bread is a bite of sin. Everything that grows among infidels is sin, every plant, every piece of meat! Sin that you'll imbibe!

I have observed my brothers slip into trousers, closely, I'll be able to do it once I'm holding a pair of jeans in my hands.

Yunus has found work in Austria. And a flat.

Three passports, four airplane tickets, four visas. Again and again, I leaf through everything, search for the photos in the passports. As long as our photos are in the passports, we're complete. Seda is registered in my passport, Seda doesn't have her own photo, Seda only has her name. I read it over and over, Seda Şahin, Seda Şahin, that's all right, you can't read it off the page, you cannot, it remains there, it's written on the page, plainly, in plain letters: Seda Şahin, Seda Şahin.

Yunus' cousin takes us to the airport, Seda, Selin, Halil and me, two suitcases, two bags, racing heartbeats and held breaths.

Four boarding passes, red and white with golden lettering, three passports, four visas held firm in hand, we enter the departure hall.

You have to go through there and then to B62.

I don't know what B62 is.

Passports!

I hand our passports through a glass window, the customs officer skims through our documents.

You had your first child out of wedlock?

No!

You had your first child when you were thirteen. You're not allowed to get married at thirteen.

I'm confused.

Come with me!

I follow him, Seda on my arm, Selin and Halil by the hand, through several swing doors into an office. Police.

I'm sitting on an orange plastic chair, both girls on my lap, Halil presses against me. We have three passports and four visas, we have photographs and Seda's name in block capitals. But there are at least two years missing in my passport, one year in Halil's, a few months in Selin's, a few days in Seda's. We're smugglers of false numbers. Because we don't have any numbers that belong to us. That's not my fault, only a father can register his children officially. The chief of police leafs through our documents.

Where are you from?

Tekbaş, I answer quietly.

The chief of police smiles, Just like my wife.

Headscarves pulled deep over my forehead, the three children on my arm and by the hand, I climb the stairs into the airplane carrying us into new freedom.

The plane carries us upwards, Turkey beneath us becomes small, finally we fly into the cheerful sky.

The plane doors open, we enter the country of blue jeans and trainers, the country of sin.

We're flowing from one floor to the next on metal stairs. Our suitcases come flowing just like us. We are being washed into a marble arena.

Yunus is leaning against a silver banister, with open arms.

The roads are smooth in the serene sky. I'm looking out the fogged car window and see women in blue jeans, with deep cleavages and free hands and arms, I see wafting hair.

Twenty square metres of hope. There are curtains on a silver curtain rail. They have a yellow and blue chequered pattern. There's a big bed in which Yunus, Seda and I are going to sleep and a smaller one for Selin and Halil. There are two bedside tables and two bedside lamps with yellow shades. There's a table, on it a tablecloth with blue sea shells and two chairs.

Yunus leaves in the morning and comes back in the evening. He works. For four days. Then he leaves for three days.

For thirty days and nights, we only leave the room to go to the bathroom that we share with strangers we never see.

We occupy ourselves, play with five marbles that the children were given on the airplane.

A tree is in bloom outside the window. It's an apple tree.

There's a knock. Strange words come through the keyhole, I don't dare to open the door.

The knock returns. Every day. Always at the same time. The same words. The strange voice sounds warm. It's old and belongs to a woman. I risk it and open the door a tiny crack, something is being reached through, chocolate, wrapped in silver foil, it smells of nuts and raisins, I close the door. Every day something else is stretched out towards us through the cracked door. Chocolate with nuts, apples, chewing gum.

After thirty days, I take the children firmly by the hand and for the first time, we leave the twenty square metres of hope. We sneak down the stairs, crouching like dogs with their tails between their legs. We venture ahead step by step, into the strange territory.

We're standing timidly on a stretch of grass in front of the house and try to smile into the foreign land. We're quiet. Only briefly one of the children leaps across the grass, but turns back immediately.

When Yunus comes home, we're long since back in our room.

The German language surges outside our door.

When we dare to venture from the twenty square metres of hope, the children and I float at its surface, dead man. We don't know what's beneath us, we float between the foreign language and the serene sky.

That's when I throw Turkish words in front of the children's feet, stepping stones, I build them a path with Turkish sentences, string together Turkish sentence to Turkish sentence, Turkish word to Turkish word.

Dikkat. Sevgilim. Bağırma.

The children jump from stone to stone.

When we return to our room, the German words ring in our ears, they are caught in our hair, and it happens more and more that one of us has a German word on their tongue. That scares the others.

We gather around the blossoming apple tree like sheep. An old woman is standing behind the fence, she waves at us. She has a small, yellow book in her hand, she flips through it and throws a Turkish question over the fence:

İsmin ne?

She hands me the yellow book through the pickets, then her hand, as well as the German language, piece by piece.

I am. You are. I go. You come. My name is Filiz. I have three children.

I absorb the words, learn quickly, from now on I get my small ration daily.

When Yunus is gone, we go for walks with Johanna and her granddaughter. Johanna has a backpack filled with German words, all of them neatly wrapped in parchment paper, there are some for the children as well. Picnic in the shade. The Danube flows by, greenly. The children beckon quacking ducks with bread crumbs and try to touch them, they are wild animals.

Halil and Selin take Johanna's granddaughter by the hand, they swing her through the air, play her favourite game, One, two, three, whee! When we return to the room, the sun stands in our eyes, our cheeks are red.

One evening, Yunus holds out a key to me like a treasure. The innkeeper, the owner of the house, gave it to Yunus. I'm allowed to clean the inn and the kitchen on the ground floor.

After hours, long past midnight, I enter the inn.

The emptiness is neon white. The hands that held the dirty knives have gone, just as the lips that pulled the meat off the smudgy forks, the mouths into which the food disappeared off the plates, sticky with remnants of sauces and ketchup stains, just as the bodies, whose warmth still clings to the chairs. The last voices have taken their coats off the hooks. The doors have snapped shut. I am alone.

I roll up my sleeves. I grab the dirty paper napkins lying on and underneath the benches and clear the half-full glasses off the table. Again and again, money falls into my hands, coins, worn, all of them, I collect them and put them into a freshly washed ashtray that I set down on the counter.

At two o'clock in the morning, I enter the kitchen. I scrub the burnt-in fat off the tiles with wire wool. Coldness spills from the walk-in refridgerator behind the heavy, shiny silver door, I mop the floor, clean the stove, the deep fat fryer, the grill and the oven. The emptiness has been scrubbed clean when I walk back up the stairs.

I sleep for two hours, then I get up to make breakfast for Yunus and the children.

At midnight, I sneak out of our flat again, down into the neon-white emptiness. There is an envelope lying on the counter, my name written on it.

I clean all night through.

The next morning, I place the envelope onto Yunus' plate, unopened. He opens it while chewing and counts the money.

She likes you, she gave you more than we agreed to, good. He nods at me and puts the money into his wallet.

I live in Austria now. Meat is meat in Austria. Chicken is chicken. In Austria, you don't have to wait for a chicken to come flying out of nowhere. I take it from the cooling shelves in the supermarket. Magnificently wrapped, the chickens are lying on magnificent shelves in magnificent markets. I glide across the smooth floor with a shopping trolley. Peach juice, carrot juice, orange juice, cherry juice and grapefruit juice. Multivitamin juice. Varieties of sausage and cheese. The shelves filled with white bread, round as well as angular, as a whole loaf or cut, to be baked at home or be toasted, coffee beans, ground or whole, from Africa, Brazil, Indonesia, pudding with strawberry, peach, or mango flavour, cream, fat, low fat, butter, salted and sweet, from Ireland, France or Austria, milk, Landliebe, Bärenmarke, soy milk, formula, Heumilch. I want to take everything. I want to give my children everything. Of all of it. Everything. This is Austria. This is Europe. I grab Austria with both hands and stack it into my trolley: Austria in bulk.

While Yunus waits in his shiny car in front of the supermarket, I push the trolley across the car park and put Austria into the trunk.

Yunus is looking for a fight. He's searching my bags, my clothes, rummages through the children's clothes, digs around in the dresser, looks underneath the carpet, in every bag, in the porridge oats, in the fridge, in the jam jar for something he can take offence at, he ravages the flat, then he grips my head, digs through my thoughts.

You're talking badly about me! With whom? With the Austrian woman?

He looks underneath my tongue.

He throws me onto my back and spreads my legs.

Do you desire another man?

With both hands, he rummages around inside my hole, examines my desire, searches for another man. When he doesn't find anything he can take offence at, he opens his trousers and takes me.

There's a knock, the landlady yells, kicks the door, saviour.

Yunus dashes to the door, yanks it open, the landlady screams:

Enough! You have to move out!

Yunus grabs her by the shoulders, shakes her, wants to beat her, stops, kicks the door shut and beats me.

When I regain consciousness, we have one week to vacate the flat.

With packed suitcases and the children by the hand, I'm standing at Johanna's fence, the only place I don't have to expect a fight.

The new flat used to be a cowshed. The floor is damp like the walls, water seeps in through the burst walls, a few weeks ago, the Danube was flowing through this room. With the flood, the flies came, Danube pebbles on the windowsill, algae-like growth sticking to the doorframe. The walls are slimy, the stench is hardly bearable, this has to be a mistake. Austria! Europe!

But an orchard stretches out in front of the damp cave and behind it, the Danubian wetlands begin. Nature is a paradise. Here, I can go outside with the children. Here, Yunus can beat me undisturbed. Here, nobody hears us. Two thousand five hundred Schilling a month, to us, it's worth it.

I chop wood and carry the logs. In order to dry the flat before winter comes, I fire up all three ovens for weeks. I frequently re-paint the flaking walls. We live wall to wall with the cows, we hear their chains rattling and their hooves hitting the feeding trough. I buy milk from the farmer's wife who owns the flat. I make butter, yogurt and cheese our way, Yunus wants the taste of Turkey. At four in the morning, I prepare the cream for breakfast, bake flatbread and cook lunch, which Yunus is going to take to work with him. We have beds, all five of us, a table with chairs and a sofa from the flea market, a flower vase, a red, embroidered tablecloth and freshly painted walls. We even have a television set. Just outside the front door, nature stretches out, lush green and fruit trees with crooked branches. They are heavily laden with fruit. Apples, pears, quince and plums in the grass, wasps buzzing around them. Sometimes I walk barefoot through the grass and lie down among the burst plums. Bejewelled in blue, I lie among the blue fruit.

The farmer's wife takes Halil and me to school and then she takes Selin and me to kindergarten. The teachers talk to me and smile at me, I don't understand them, I nod, they put their arms around my children's shoulders and lead them from the room.

In the mornings, I am now alone with Seda.

Halil and Selin bring bills home from school and from kindergarten, for the field trip and the school milk. Soon they are blue and burst open like plums in the grass.

For days, they don't go to school and to kindergarten.

The farmer's wife gives me a stretch of the garden. I lay out a vegetable patch. This is where everything we need to live shall grow.

The farmer's wife is happy about the manicured garden and the cleaned carpet that's hanging out to dry in front of the house. She goes into the stable to take a look at her cows and at us. In the mornings and in the evenings.

Once, she leaves a warm jacket for Halil hanging on the door. Then there's a jug of milk on the threshold. I hang baklava on the fence for her.

The farmer takes Halil along on his tractor. Together they muck out the stables and examine the fishponds. When he comes home, Halil has meadows in his eyes. His gait is upright, his forehead smooth.

He calls the farmer Grandpa.

Selin and Halil bring excitement home from school and from kindergarten, Saint Nicholas is coming, Saint Nicholas is coming!

I don't know Saint Nicholas, watch the children's excitement like somebody who can't swim watches swimmers frolicking in a lake. The farmer's wife asks me if Saint Nicholas can come to our house. Yunus approves. I don't know if he knows Saint Nicholas.

The children are drenched in excitement and joy. I'm standing there swathed in my veils, not a single toe touching the water.

I'm firing up the oven when there's a knock on the door. Yunus opens it. A woman comes in, with a long, fake white beard, her mouth is invisible, she is wearing a tall, stiff hat made from paper. A red floor-length coat. White cotton in her eyebrows. Strands of cotton across her eyes.

She's veiled like I am.

She has a big burlap sack with her and asks the children if they have been good. Halil and Selin recite a poem with hasty breath. Rhymes as clear as glass that I don't know and don't understand. The children receive presents, chocolate, apples, tangerines and nuts. Selin is given gloves, Seda gets socks and Halil a pencil case. Selin and Halil sing a song, quietly and timidly.

Morgen Kinder, wird's was geben, morgen werden wir uns freuen.

I'm standing still. Wide-eyed and speechless. I don't know what is going to happen tomorrow. My children are pulling ahead of me, they are strong swimmers.

The excitement grows. The children say it's Advent.

Each day, they open a small door on a large piece of cardboard with a colourful design and twenty-four doors, an Advent calendar the children say, which Selin was given as a gift from a girl at school. When they've opened the last door, they stand at the kitchen window and wait, all day long, I don't know what for, for the *Christkind*, they say, whom I don't know, and who apparently comes down from the sky. They're unwilling to leave the window for even a moment, I want to disperse their hope carefully to spare them the disappointment, Come, Selin, Come, Halil, but the children aren't deterred, they stay by the window, the *Christkind* is coming!

There's a knock, the front door is pushed open before I'm able to open it, the farmer's wife and her daughter carry in a Christmas tree, decorated in red and gold, they put it in the centre of the living room, light the candles and sparkling sticks hanging off its branches, sparks land on the presents lying underneath the branches, the children squeeze through the door and stand still, the Christmas tree reflected in their eyes, they're nothing but light and presents now, nothing but *Christkind*.

Thanks be to Allah! Three little *Christkinder*.

The farmer's wife and her daughter sing a song, *Silent night, holy night, All is calm, all is bright, Round yon virgin mother and child, Holy infant, so tender and mild*, Selin and Halil sing along, quietly and brightly.

I am standing knee-deep in strange waters, they're warm. I'm filled with wonder and wade deeper, up to my chest.

Selin receives a Barbie doll. She grabs it tightly in her hand all throughout the evening. Halil is lying on the floor and flips through a book about dinosaurs. Only Seda leaves her xylophone lying in the corner.

We eat börek and baklava. We laugh. Boldly. A number of times.

The children. Yunus. And I.

Then the farmer's wife and her daughter go home. The darkness is full of snow and fog. Goodbye, Nanna!

Yunus is silent.

Lying in bed later, I thank Allah for this Christmas Eve. And I thank Nanna.

I'm talking on the phone with my mother.

Filiz, she says quietly, Filiz.

For weeks, she hasn't been going down to the village or down the street, doesn't leave the house after nightfall, not even to go to the toilet in the yard. My father locks the door, then he crawls, chamber pot in his hand and joins my mother under the table. They don't dare to go to their bed, that's the spot they shoot at first.

The PKK invades the village, flags flying.

The star sits inside the circle, the fire is inside the star, my mother says quietly.

Mummy, I whisper, Mummy.

The war interrupts the connection.

Yunus' suits are made from silk, shiny, they fit his shiny silver car with leather seat covers, his leather wallet, the heavy watch and the golden necklace. When he stands next to me, fragrant, his curls black and shiny with hair lacquer, the sunglasses sitting on his face, I am nothing. My feet are clad in socks I crocheted myself and brown plastic sandals, I'm wearing the old skirt and the blouse with the faded flowers. Yunus' fingernails are polished, he's now wearing a big ring. I have forgotten my hair, which has long since stopped falling in curls underneath my headscarf. Strange, the fact that he still pushes inside me. What business does the dick of a man with black sunglasses have underneath my old skirt?

The fingers with the polished nails and the big ring caress Seda's and Selin's hair. The girls are pretty, even in the dresses with the fabric worn thin in some places.

Then we're standing at the front door and watch the silver car drive away.

He earns twenty-five thousand Schilling a month, nanna whispers, standing next to me at the stove, plus the child benefit. Yunus buys and sells houses and flats, real estate, buys a house in Istanbul, an flat in Antalya, then he sells both!

Where is the money?

I don't know, I say and knead the dough.

Yunus is our weather.

He freezes the young buds off the branches, he hails spring out of our limbs and our heads.

Nanna is crying, I implore her to keep calm.

She checks on the cows when Yunus comes home from work.

What's the weather like?, she asks. Cloudy, I reply.

Is there a storm coming?

I don't answer, I don't want to know Nanna in the stable, wall to wall with me, when Yunus beats me or pushes into me.

I'm not allowed to go shopping for food on my own any more. Yunus accompanies me to the supermarket. He keeps an eye on me, even walking along the shelves with vinegar and oil. My gaze remains lowered, to the wheels of the shopping trolley, to the gaps between the floor tiles, I glance only at rice, fried batter pearls and pasta.

At the end of the aisles, I hear a number and put the money down on a plastic tray. I see a man's hand take the money off the tray and tie my gaze to the tray like a dog to a peg. I wait obediently for the man's hand to put the change onto the tray. I take it and look back towards the floor.

Gaps, gaps, gaps up to Yunus' shoes. Yunus takes the money from my hand and checks it to the last penny.

When I give Nanna the two thousand five hundred Schilling for rent, she sometimes hands five hundred back to me. For me and the children.

She buys fabric and yarn for me, and I embroider tablecloths with blossoms, and she sells them for me.

When Yunus notices, he takes the money.

I become smarter and practice lying, become better and better at lying, I lie into the mirror, lie to the children to train myself, I lie without a racing heartbeat, without my cheeks blushing, with open eyes and lids that don't twitch any more.

I keep the notes between the cleaning rags. And coins, gold and silver.

With them, I pay the bills from school and kindergarten, I buy peace and quiet for us, I redeem the children from beatings and if I have money left, myself as well.

I calculate with precision. I always hold back a few coins. It's better that Selin receives a few hits, so that I can keep a reserve fund in case of a catastrophe.

In my head, I keep an account of all incomes and all expenses, the bought peace, the prevented and the unprevented hits.

How many hits for me equal one hit for the children, how many hits equal how many thrusts, how much is the prevention of a beating, how much the prevention of rape.

I calculate using my own measuring units. The smallest unit is the hit. The hits on back and hip, on arms and legs are one point each, hits to the stomach and the fingers are two points each, hits to the head and into the face are four each, if they are carried out with a piece of wood, I double the points, if it's metal, it's four times as many, rape counts for eight points.

Lists of earnings, lists of expenses, lists of levies.

Once, Halil breaks an alarm clock while playing. How many hits for whom? Fifteen for Halil or maybe just ten? Thirty hits for me or ten hits and fifteen thrusts? I'm not sure about the number of hits, I'm certain about the thrusts. How much is an alarm clock, how much of a cushion do I have left, time is of the essence, I reach for the money between the rags and run to nanna, she leaves and buys an alarm clock.

The new alarm clock is ticking.

When Yunus comes home, he doesn't notice anything.

Tonight, it stays quiet.

In the afternoons, I delve into telenovelas. Klaus becomes my husband, and Adrian and Bianca are my children. My company is doing badly, it's on the verge of bankruptcy. It was my mistake, letting my brother take a share of the company, I'm suspecting one of my sister-in-law's schemes behind it.

Who knows what a woman does with the driving instructor in the car.

Every night, the driver's license is Yunus' topic, the crazy asshole-men, the whores behind the wheel. Each night, his voice becomes sharper, and when it has become razor-sharp, he enrols me for driving classes.

I'm sitting in a big room and learn about right of way. Yunus is sitting in the hallway and waits. I do not lift my eyes off the Turkish book, do not make eye contact with the Turkish teacher.

Compulsory waiting. If, at a crossroads, signs regulate right of way, or if there is a stop sign, one is obligated to give way to the other drivers coming from both the left and the right. At a stop sign, the vehicle must be stopped completely in any case. Yet a sign regulating right of way may be amended by a sign carrying instructions for a special procedure which must be heeded. I barely dare to breathe, Yunus in the hallway, Yunus breathing down my neck. Vehicles in flowing traffic have right of way before vehicles coming from slip roads, residential streets, or out of driveways. Cyclists leaving the bike lane must give priority to flowing traffic. Vehicles on slip roads have right of way before vehicles coming from residential streets or out of driveways. I hear Yunus' steps. If a vehicle is moving on a major road, it has right of way before all other vehicles, even if those want to turn onto the crossroads from the right.

Clad in deep blue I fall asleep.

I study among the laundry and the children. Give priority to vehicles from the opposite direction. Seda is crying, she bumped into something, I put my hand on her forehead. No overtaking. Seda's tears trickle down between lorries and flowing traffic.

I don't know any woman who learns as quickly, the driving instructor commends me to Yunus.

Yunus breaks my ring finger.

You're driving.

I sit down on the driver's seat, stare ahead. The children on the back seat are dead silent. The Danube is flowing only a few metres from the bumper. The wheel is damp.

Yunus blindfolds me.

The children have stopped breathing.

I hear the river flowing.

Yunus turns the key in the ignition, release the clutch slowly!

I release the clutch slowly.

Step on the gas!

I step on the gas. The engine revs, dies, Yunus' fist drives into my face.

Yunus turns the key in the ignition, release the clutch slowly!

I release the clutch slowly.

Step on the gas!

I step on the gas. The engine revs, dies, Yunus' fist drives into my face.

Yunus turns the key in the ignition, release the clutch slowly!

I release the clutch slowly.

Step on the gas! I step on the gas. The engine revs, dies, Yunus' fist drives into my face.

Finally, the car starts moving.

Put your foot down! Down! Down!

I put my foot down, I speed up, towards the Danube.

Put your foot down! Down! Down!

I jerk the wheel violently, Yunus' fist drives into my face.

Don't turn the wheel without my command!

The engine dies, Yunus is laughing at me, my mouth is filled with blood.

The driving instructor picks me up. Yunus has arranged it. He's standing at the window. I put on my veils. Yunus opens the front door for the driving instructor. I go with the strange man. Yunus stares out the window. Underneath his gaze, I get into the strange car.

My life is in the driving instructor's hands.

His smile at the goodbye, and I am dead.

But maybe it's his life in my hands as well, my smile at the goodbye, and he is dead.

I don't know what the driving instructor looks like. I don't know if he is short or tall. I try to turn my ears away from his voice. I don't make a sound. Gear box. Thirty kmph. Full beam. Dip the headlights. Turn the headlights on full. I drive like I'm in a trance.

Six weeks later, I am to take my driving test.

Yunus turns to stone when I get into the car with four men. The driving instructor, two men from the assessment commission, the interpreter, Yunus breathing down my neck!

No glance at any of the men, no sound, no gesture. With a trembling hand, I turn the key in the ignition,

I hear the river flowing, hear Yunus' voice: Release the clutch slowly!

I release the clutch slowly.

Step on the gas!

I step on the gas. The engine revs, dies, keep calm, the driving instructor says. I turn the key in the iginition, I'm trembling, keep calm, Mrs Şahin, keep calm. Jumpily, we start driving.

I have to reverse into a parking space.

The car is at a right angle. The men get out of the car.

My head sinks to the steering wheel.

The interpreter opens the car door.

You passed, Mrs Şahin!

Yunus is pacing in front of the driving school. When I get out of the car, his jaw is taunt and his hand is ready.

I passed.

Yunus looks at me in disbelief.

I'm proud of you!

I can send my wife to take driving lessons. I can trust my wife. Now the assholes are quiet, Yunus says.

Yunus' Mercedes drives up. The closing of the car door determines my fear, it's the sound of his fury. He comes to the front door, I open the door for him, and in passing, he kicks the steel toe-cap of his boot against my shin. I see glaring, colourful stars. Acute, sharp pain.

The children duck, they hunch their shoulders, form a herd to stand against the wolf, huddle together, the youngest lamb in the middle. Against the father. The master over everything.

I crouch down at his feet, unlace his boots, take them off, put his slippers on his feet and we go to the bathroom, I take off his shirt, trousers, socks, and underwear, shower him, lather him, rub him, dry him, help him into fresh clothes. He eats, his meat, his rice, his cake, drinks his coffee, and if he is so inclined, he orders me to bed.

Satisfied, he lies there.

With a bucket full of water, I go outside to his Mercedes. I wipe down the shiny mahogany dashboard, the steering wheel, the soft leather seats, I pull the long, blonde hairs from the gaps in between the seats, pick them up from underneath the footmats, and collect the filled condoms in a plastic bag. Then I go back to the children.

I'm sitting in front of the pile of wood in the kitchen, look for the round logs, and pile them to the top. Round wood creates bruises, wood with edges also rips the skin.

I'm lying on the kitchen floor and am beaten out of my body. Yunus is drenched in sweat, the wood in his hand, caught in the rhythm of his blows, he doesn't see me any more. I know that the children are listening in the next room, listen to the beatings their father administers, to their mother's screams.

Yunus is exhausted, his arm is tired. He kneels down, lifts me up, lies me on the kitchen bench, unbuttons my blouse, exposes my blue chest, pushes my skirt up and fucks me.

I'm standing in the airport, I'm coming to you.

Mother is here. My mother. She surprises me, out of the serene blue.

For three months, my mother is allowed to stay with me. That's what it says on the visa.

My mother carries the war in her eyes.

War veteran.

I want to cry in her arms, but I don't dare burden her with myself.

Until late into the night, Mother tells me about the war.

I hear laughter in the garden. A Turkish girl has trampled the grass beneath the fruit trees. Yunus goes across the trampled grass and puts his hand down the girl's skirt. I hear giggling from between the branches.

My mother and I are standing at the window.

Leave it, I say.

Every night, the Turkish girl now tramples my grass.

As long as her whooping and moaning comes from the garden, Yunus doesn't push into me at night.

Mother is sitting on the stairs in front of the house, I'm watering my vegetables.

Who do you love more, your mother or me?

I love you both, Yunus.

Yunus runs his hand through the courgette plants, he feels the fruit, weighs them in his hand, plucks one, the evening light is golden, he whacks my face with it.

Only thought: Mother! I try to hide the beaten daughter behind the bushes, but Mother comes running towards me.

No, Mummy, don't!

Yunus pulls me into the house by my hair and throws me against the edge of the bed.

It's quiet. Darkness. Stars in all sorts of colours, spinning around me, solar system. I see Yunus hitting the body in which I no longer am, with slow, dancer-like movements.

Mother throws herself in front of Yunus.

Stop, I beg of you, don't kill her!

Yunus turns away from me and thrashes my mother against the wall.

For the second time, I am born from my mother's pain.

Mother and I sleep the dead sleep of blue women.

Thank you very much, Mother says, for everything. She is flying back to Turkey today.

You have to give your husband more love, or else you're going to lose him. What will become of the children then.

I am soundless and colourless and timeless, I care neither about the children nor the roses and the ripe plums in the garden, nor about the static on the radio. I sit in the garden, I don't feel the rain that has set in.

Up on one leg!

Halil and Selin are standing next to each other, on one leg.

Kneel!

Seda kneels, Yunus pushes a lighter into her hand.

If a foot touches the ground, burn them! Seda is crying, Yunus is laughing. For a long time, the children stand upright, then Selin loses her balance, she staggers, the foot she had lifted touches the floor. Yunus yells: Burn her! Seda is crying, Yunus hits her on the back of her head, twice. Burn her! A flame shoots up, Seda holds it underneath Selin's twitching foot and burns her sister. Selin screams with pain. The lighter falls from Seda's hand. Seda rolls towards me, kicked by her father, a piece of dirt, comes to a halt before my feet, and doesn't move, her eyes are closed. I lift her eyelids, the eyeball is white. Seda! Seda!

Seda comes to, looks at me, big eyes, as though she was coming from a different star, as though I had brought her back to us unjustly.

Death is talking to me.

It moves the knife into my line of sight, and puts the rope in my hand, it opens the medicine cabinet and reads the leaflets with information about the medicine to me.

My sinews are showing clearly, my arteries are not. I don't have a bathtub, but there are more than enough beams.

I ask Yunus about the Turkish girl.

She wants to marry me, Yunus says, but you're staying.

No, I say for the first time.

No.

I am pushed against the wall, Yunus' arm floating above me, a hammer in his hand.

One more word, and I'll split you in half.

Yunus' legs are itchy. I wash them, put ointment on them. The next day, they are red, spotty, swollen. Pus, dark yellow and thick, a worm crawls out of a festering sore. I pull at its head with tweezers, the worm is long. The outline of a second is visible underneath the thin, red skin of the sore.

Yunus is pushing into me, worms in his leg.

My skin begins to itch, then the children's skin does too.

I wrap the worm in tinfoil and take it to the doctor in the village. I show the worm to the nurse. I admit that it comes from Yunus.

But please tell the doctor that it comes from me.

She gives me medicine. When I reach out my hand, my blue bracelet flashes briefly from underneath the sleeve, the nurse sees it, I flinch backwards, the medicine falls to the ground. She pushes me into the treatment room and locks the door behind us. She takes my hand, pushes up the sleeve, then my dress, the shades of blue on my body iridescent.

I fell.

She doesn't say a word. I'm grateful that she doesn't believe me.

There's a women's shelter, the nurse says.

Words like protection and calm, support, safety, help float around me like glistening bubbles. Doesn't she know that Yunus would charge into any house? Kill the children? Kill me? The women in the shelter? With the kitchen knife?

And if he doesn't charge into the house, he will lie in wait, as soon as I leave the shelter, he will cut my throat, he will hang me up by my feet, and skin me, he will gut me, heart, spleen, soul, brain, he will eat my liver and mount my head to the wall. Doesn't she know that? Doesn't she know the world? Doesn't she know that the world belongs to Yunus?

I am obligated to report your husband to the police, the doctor says.

The only option I have left: Taking my children and escaping to Turkey. To my family.

The doctor's wife has bought us four plane tickets to Istanbul.

Tomorrow, when Yunus has left the house, Nanna is going to take us to the airport.

Racing heart. I pack the suitcases secretly. When the children come home, I smile. I'm not going to tell them, the risk is too high. Check the clock.

Selin and Halil are playing in the garden. I'm alone in the children's room with a packed suitacse and my decision, with danger and the risk. I hear the children laughing in the garden. For the first time in a long while.

Yunus comes home. I avoid his gaze and think about the suitcase underneath the children's bed. The passports. The tickets. My treasure. Flight pulsing in my veins. Freedom. In each room I now walk into, there's Yunus. Yunus is sitting, standing, lying everywhere. He calls me to him, more often than usual? Check the clock. We have to wind ourselves through the hands of the clock, I have to shove the children through a window in time.

The clock ticks while Yunus pushes into me.

All night long, my heartbeat thunders. The children breathe steadily, Yunus is sleeping, only I and my decision are awake, danger and risk.

Then the alarm clock rings into my sleeplessness. Now that the decision is made, it takes over command and fuels me. I get up, prepare Yunus' breakfast one more time, bake flatbread the way he likes it, add honey to his yogurt, jam on the table, sausage, cheese, the way he wants it, I spread butter onto his bread. Lunchbox and thermos at the ready. I don't dare to rush Yunus. I sit at the table and wait. Check the clock. The seconds go by loudly.

When Yunus comes, he sits down at the table, still half-asleep. He lets me pour his coffee, milk, stir in the sugar.

In the dawn, I can make out the outlines of the dark grey car outside. Our escape car. It's parked at the end of the path. Check the clock.

Time goes by.

At last, Yunus puts the napkin down on the table, I jump up, want to go to the bathroom with him.

Leave it, he says, I'm not going to work today.

Either you kill yourself now, or I'll hang you, in front of the children. Yunus leaves the room, slams the door behind him.

Our plane tickets are lying on the table, ripped up, the contents of the suitcase strewn across the floor, the passports burnt in the sink, blood drips from my nose.

I pick up Seda and Selin, carry them to their room, put them down on their bed. They are silent and put up no resistance. I pull the covers over them, lock their hands with each other. I kiss them on the forehead. I beckon Halil, come! Halil lies down next to his sisters, he too is silent and without resistance. I interlace his fingers with the girls' fingers. I kiss my son on his forehead.

The children's eyes are black holes.

I leave. A step.

Seda cries quietly.

Mummy! Stay!

A step.

Sleep now.

Walk into the Danube, all the way down to the riverbed, until I am muddy, until I float on the surface bloated, gaze into the waves beyond death, and then, saturated, sink back down to the bottom.

Seda. Selin. Halil. What will become of you?

Mummy is at the bottom of the Danube.

Jump in head first?

Stones in the pockets!

My skirt doesn't have pockets. Make a knot with the skirt, fill it with stones. Not a lot of small ones. Just one big one. Search. This one. Yes. This one is going to drag me to the bottom of the river. Heavy. Sit down. Spread my legs. Roll the stone into my lap. Tie the skirt above the stone. A tight knot, one that won't loosen.

Finally. Peace. Silence.

Bright brawl.

Mrs Şahin!

My bed is soft and warm.

Mrs Şahin! Can you hear me?

I open my eyes.

A doctor is talking to me, as though he was allowed to. As though he weren't a man. And I weren't a woman. He smiles at me. I'm lying in front of him, scarfless. And no beating for it. My lips are slow. As is my tongue. And my thoughts. Fear cowers in my head, too tired to stir, tired dog.

You need to sleep.

Lying down. Sleeping. Resting. The white of the walls. A day. A night.

Spring is hanging above the bed. Japanese cherry blossoms. Lush branches in a wooden frame. Fragrance behind the glass. Frozen spring.

I stare at the blossoms and push myself behind the glass. In the hallway, suddenly, children's footsteps. Halil, Seda, Selin. Walking, running, standing. They are coming from the battlefield.

I hold my breath.

They mustn't find me!

Logs of wood are lying atop and across one another, these splintered, shattered, those ready. The pitchfork's prongs are standing in rank and file.

Yunus' heavy boots trample the grass, and the rope is hanging from the sky above it.

We want to see our mummy!

My rope is dangling in the wind. None of the children wants to hang for me.

The door opens, a small slit in the whiteness.

Mrs Şahin, your children are here.

I shake my head.

And shut my eyes.

The deep-sea anglerfish is able to create light for itself. I can't light my own way any longer. I can't be light.

Not even in my dreams. I'm too tired for dreams. They have forgotten me, they don't come any more.

Dreamless sleep.

Silence.

Downs are growing in my head, white, soft, fluffy.

Mrs Şahin!

I push my head into the pillow.

Downs in my head. Downs in my head.

Mrs Şahin!

There is someone behind the mountains, calling.

Mrs Şahin! Your children are here.

I turn my head to the wall, eyes shut tight, like iron gates.

No children! No blue children! No cries from the battlefield! No blue!

Downs in my head. Downs in my head. White, soft and fluffy. White, white. I want to breathe whiteness. Whiteness is what I want to drink, and whiteness is what I want to eat.

Downs in my head. Downs in my head. They are my wings. I want to crawl under them.

No children!

When the nurse with the red glasses invades my whiteness, a golden cross around her neck, when she yanks open the windows, such wonderful weather, pulls the blanket off my legs and leaves me lying in my bed naked, featherless, no downs, is when I'm scared of falling from the nest. Because she brings time, the fussy nurse. Because she comes, the days go by. And time will bring blue children to the bed: Halil, Seda, Selin.

Mummy!

Downs in my head.

Mummy!

I keep the iron gates shut.

Girly fingers pry them open.

Mummy!

The battlefield is reflected in Selin's eyes.

Come home, Mummy! Come! Daddy is crying. Daddy needs you!

Seda's hand lying on top of mine. Underneath her sleeve, a bracelet, blue as the summer sky, flashes.

Mummy!

Downs in my head and in my mouth.

Mummy!

The children bejewelled in blue on both sides of the bed.

Words are falling from their blue lips onto my white bed. The children fetch my shoes, small fingers grab my feet, put them into the shoes, tie up the laces, Seda's fingers manage a bow. Daddy needs you! Selin combs my hair, ties it up, pulls the headscarf over my forehead, hides the hair, ties the scarf underneath my chin. Come home! Halil props me up, puts my coat around me, the girls button it up, smooth out the wrinkles, the three of them together rip a hole into my whiteness and drag me to the door.

While the cat's away, the mice will play. The girls shine with their mother's blue jewellery. Seda is wearing my bracelet, it shines darkly, too dark for her. Selin has put my tiara into her hair.

Staggering, supported by blue children, I walk towards the battlefield. Suddenly, the red glasses with the golden cross stand in front of the frosted-glass door. She puts her hands on my shoulders, Mrs Şahin, you can't leave yet! The frosted-glass door opens without making a sound, and I see, upright and tall:

Yunus.

Mrs Şahin, you can't leave yet!

Yunus is my magnet.

Flowers in front of his chest.

Rose buds, dark yellow sunflowers, camomiles and hyacinths.

Yunus holds out his blooming meadow towards me, I fall into his arms, they are strong and warm, I can feel his muscles, veins and sinews, my dry lips on his salty tears.

Forgive me! Forgive me!

His eyes are green. From the river?

You're my star!

His voice is without any doubt.

You're mine.

In the rustling of the black Mercedes, in the fragrance of the flowers, my hand tightly in his.

You're my place. I'm meant for you.

The children on the backseat keep still in their mother's blue jewellery.

In front of our house, Yunus opens the car door, he lifts me from the car and carries me through the garden. I see the Turkish girl's footprints in the grass.

Heavy boots in the entrance.

Yunus carries me over the threshold.

Bride me.

This time, I'm allowed into the house without shards. No clapping, no yelling.

My dress isn't too long, but still I don't have hands.

I'm fluttering among the branches on the holy tree and am still carrying my wish.

Yunus sets me down on the bed carefully.

In his arms, sleep comes over me.

I'm lying in the blackness of the night and listen to the rhythm of faded blows.

Blow. After blow. Blow. After blow.

On this bed. Against this wall. On this floor.

Blow. After blow. Blow. After blow.

The old blows echo.

My pulse is their echo.

Yunus is kneeling next to me.

You'll never laugh again. Never. Just as well. No one but me is going to see your lips, your open mouth.

Just as well.

His fingers trace across my face tenderly.

You are mine. Completely. Finally. Mine.

Yunus' tongue caresses my mouth.

Racing pulse.

Blow. After blow. Blow. After blow.

When I wake up the next morning, Yunus is sitting by my bed.

His eyes across mine, his hand on my forehead.

His voice is swooshing around in my blood, you have to drink. He has brought me mint tea.

Is this the world again? This time in green?

With honey. The spoon knocking against the glass. Drink.

The world tastes bitter, drips down from the corners of my mouth.

Another sip, Filiz.

Flowing from the corner of my mouth.

Drink. You need to drink.

My lips seal.

Then my eyelids, and I sink back into sleep.

You have to drink!

Murmuring voices.

The echo of faded blows in my blood.

Blow. After blow. Blow. After blow.

Mummy!

The children knock at the door, I don't answer, still they enter, sit down at the side of my bed, take my hands, kiss my forehead and play with my feet. They put pigeon feathers between my toes. Pigeon feathers tickle the soles of my feel, with felt tip pens they paint my lips red.

Mummy!

They lift my eyelids gingerly, and hold out the pictures they have drawn towards me. I'm standing underneath a large sun, smiling from ear to ear. My garden is filled with blossoming flowers. Huge courgettes.

I have seen Japanese cherry blossoms and pushed myself behind the glass to join them.

Blow. After blow. Blow. After blow.

Sometimes I hear Seda crying. Sometimes Selin. Sometimes Halil.

I don't get up. I don't go down the stairs.

I don't stir the pots on the stove. The oven stays cold.

I don't bake bread for the children.

I don't eat.

I don't drink.

I don't know what the children eat and drink.

Blow. After blow. Blow. After blow.

I beg of you, Filiz, please, get up! I need you! The children!

Yunus opens the window, fluffs up the duvet. He grabs me underneath my armpits and changes my position as though he wanted to rearrange my limbs.

He takes the full tea glass from the nightstand, as though I had emptied it, brings a new one, as though I were able to drink.

He can't do what the red glasses could, the golden cross. Yunus, you're not bringing days into this night. Time does not flow because you come.

I won't return to being.

The door is pushed open. I hear children's footsteps.

I hear Seda's breath.

Seda, you cannot penetrate this night.

Seda's head is lying on my chest, firmly, her unwashed hair on my lips.

She takes my arm, puts it around her neck, she pushes her legs between mine.

Mummy!

Leave it, you won't get close to me.

Mummy!

She lies like this for a long time, then she sneaks out from under my body and jumps up. Mummy is dead! Mummy is dead!

Yunus rushes to my bed, he takes my head in his hands.

Wake up, wake up!

His fingers burn on my cheeks.

Filiz! Filiz!

Yunus places a piece of blue fabric across my body.

Silver buttons glisten.

Jeans? Are those jeans?

The fabric lies motionless and limp on the back of my hand.

Coarse and cold. Like me.

I have fallen from the holy tree that never existed.

I have asked for an angel that never came.

I have prayed to a God that never was.

Yunus comes flying over the hill, wolf! He attacks my motionless body, rips up my nightgown, drags it off my shoulders, my breasts, pushes it up over my hips, I'm not trembling, he spreads my legs, his spear jutting out in front of me.

He pushes into me as if he was out of his mind.

Say that you love me!

Say that you love me!

His teeth digging into my neck, his fingers sticking into my dry mouth, grabbing my lips, my teeth, my tongue, searching, his spear searches, jabs, searches for life that I don't have.

You're lying there like you're dead!

Searches, searches, searches. Searches for life.

Don't lie there like you're dead!

You want my life, Yunus, but you're my executioner.

Yunus kneels on top of me, grabs my head and pushes the spear deep into my throat, addicted to life that I don't have, deeper and deeper, pushing faster and faster, I'll suffocate!

Then a wave surges within me, gushes from my stomach, from my mouth, green foam, breaks the jabbing spear at last.

Yunus grabs the jeans, wipes the green off himself, screaming, grabs the chair and thrashes me with it.

Blow. After blow. Blow. After blow.

He shatters the nightstand, the bed frame, the children's pictures fall off the wall. He breaks my arms, my ribs.

He breaks the bridge of my nose, breaks both my jaws.

Blows are falling from the ceiling.

Blows are falling off the walls.

Blows are crawling from the gaps in the floor.

Blow. After blow. Blow. After blow.

You're beating me to death, but you won't get close to me.

The green in your eyes never came from the river.

On 1 August 1998, neighbours called an ambulance and the police to the Şahin's home. The ambulance took Filiz to the hospital; Halil, Selin and Seda were taken into custody by child-protection services.

Three months later, Filiz was released from hospital and was able to move to a women's shelter together with her children.

She divorced Yunus Şahin and adopted her maiden name.

Yunus was forbidden by the courts from having any contact with his children.

Filiz Lale began vocational training to be a chef.

After eighteen months in the women's shelter, Filiz and the children moved into their own flat.

After she finished her training, Filiz worked as a chef in a restaurant for fourteen years. While working at her job, she completed a course on psychosocial and social psychiatric therapy at the University of Klagenfurt. Today, she works as an academic professional in social psychiatry for social services in Upper Austria.

Halil trained to become a dental technician, after which he studied biology and German at the University College of Teacher Education in Vienna, and today works as a secondary-school teacher in Vienna.

After finishing high school, Selin completed a Voluntary Year of Social Service at an orphanage in Costa Rica. She went on to study Spanish and history at the University of Vienna and the Universidad de Cádiz, and is now a lecturer at a Spanish university.

Seda is head of the attorney's office at a district court in Vienna. In August 2015, she married her Turkish cousin in Istanbul who now lives with her in Austria.

Yunus Şahin returned to Istanbul after coming into conflict with the authorities in Austria.

He remarried and had three more children: Halil, Selin and Seda.